GUNFIRE

On A Quiet Street!

The Ames Hotel was on a quieter side street, which was why Harding had chosen it. There was little foot traffic here, and after a bit he tensed as he heard the distinctive footsteps which he associated with a peg leg. Without turning to look back, he cut across the street toward a pawnshop. Pretending to be interested in something in the window, he saw the reflection of the man who had been behind him. He was a complete stranger, but as Harding had surmised, he had a peg leg. Harding started to turn and face him, at the same time moving his hand toward his gun. Before he could complete the turn, the man

We will send you a free catalog on request. Any titles not in your local book store can be purchased by mail. Send the price of the book plus 50¢ shipping charge to Tower Books, P.O. Box 270, Norwalk, Connecticut 06852.

Titles currently in print are available for industrial and sales promotion at reduced rates. Address inquiries to Tower Publications, Inc., Two Park Avenue, New York, New York 10016, Attention: Premium Sales Department.

LEADVILLE

Edwin Booth

TOWER BOOKS   **NEW YORK CITY**

A TOWER BOOK

Published by

Tower Publications, Inc.
Two Park Avenue
New York, N.Y. 10016

Copyright © 1981 by Edwin Booth

Chapter One

Allan Harding, riding a sorrel, and Frisco Noonan, slouched in the saddle of a sorry-looking buckskin, rounded a curve in the road and saw the wagon up ahead. Harding, his voice muffled by a sheepskin collar which was turned up against the cold, said, "Looks like trouble for someone. Let's sit tight until we know what it's all about."

Noonan, also bundled to his ears, didn't say anything, but brought his mount to a stop. Actually, he hadn't said a great deal since leaving Central City, except to express his profane opinion of a godforsaken country that was cold enough to freeze certain portions of your anatomy. To put it mildly, which Frisco seldom did, he had no liking for cold weather.

Harding wasn't especially fond of freezing, either, but at the moment his interest was held by the tableau before them. The wagon, heavily loaded with freight, had apparently been stopped by two riders, one of whom had a carbine lying across his saddlehorn, its muzzle pointed at the driver. Words, unintelligible at this distance, indicated that a conversation was taking place, and it didn't seem to Harding that they were having a friendly chat. After watching for a few moments, he said quietly, "It appears to me the fellow on the wagon has himself outnumbered. Do you reckon we ought to deal ourselves in?"

"What I reckon don't cut much ice," Frisco said wryly, "Being as you've already made up your mind.

Besides, anything would be better than sitting here shivering. How do you figure to go about it?"

Instead of answering, Harding reached down for the carbine in his saddle scabbard, lined up the sights on a spot in the road midway between the two mounted men, and squeezed off a shot.

The reaction was just what he had expected. Both of the riders jerked their heads around to see where the shot had come from. The one with the carbine made as if to return the fire, found himself looking at the muzzle of an already leveled gun, and quickly thought better of it. He couldn't have hit anything anyway, since his horse had been spooked by the shot, and was acting up. With a curse which could be heard even at this distance, he whirled his mount and took off in the opposite direction, followed by his companion.

"Downright unsociable, ain't they," Frisco commented. "They didn't even wait to say 'howdy.' "

"Maybe they suddenly remembered someplace else where they were supposed to be," Harding said. "Anyway, I bet we'll have a chance to meet them later. Come on, let's find out what it was all about." He lifted his reins and put the sorrel into motion.

The wagon driver, who had been intent on quieting his team after the commotion, turned his head to watch them ride up. He was pretty well concealed by a long, sheepskin-lined coat, but he appeared to be tall, perhaps as tall as Harding. A heavy beard covered much of his face. Above the beard, sharp blue eyes showed no signs of fear as they watched expectantly. Harding reined up beside him.

"You seemed to be having a bit of trouble, stranger. What were those two men up to?"

"Men?" the driver scoffed. "Skunks would be a better name for them. In another ten minutes they would have dumped my load of freight down the canyon. I'd have been lucky if they didn't dump me with it. Good thing for me you came along when you did." He shifted the lines to his left hand and held out his right. "Name's Gagan, in case you're interested. My friends mostly call me Spud."

"Glad to meet you, Mr. Gagan," Allan said. "I'm Allan Harding, and my sidekick here is Frisco Noonan."

The two of them shook hands, and Gagan nodded at Frisco, who said, "These two pals of yours, I take it they don't like your looks?"

"Oh, it ain't me they don't like. Not personal, that is. It's the outfit I work for, Feeney Freight Lines. This ain't the first time they've stopped one of our wagons. I guess it won't be the last, either."

At the name "Feeney," Harding glanced quickly at Frisco, and almost imperceptibly shook his head. Frisco got the message, and kept still.

"Like I was saying," Spud continued, "It's lucky for me you came along. Not so lucky for you, though, not if you bump into the two polecats again. If it's any of my business, where are you headed for?"

"Leadville," Harding told him.

"I was afraid of that," Gagan said. "That's where they hang out. You might be smart to turn around and go back."

"Oh, I guess we'll take our chances," Harding said casually. "Between the two of us we ought to be able to handle them." He turned to look over his shoulder. "Right, Frisco?"

Frisco nodded, and said, "My pappy always told me not to let anyone buffalo me. Of course he got himself killed following his own advice, but I reckon he was right. Anyway, I sure ain't going back to that pass. I'd sooner be shot than frozen.''

"Well, it's up to you gents,'' the wagon driver said. "But there's something else you ought to know. Besides Dobbs and Faraday, them's the two you saw, you'll have half a dozen more against you. They all work for the same outfit, Rocky Mountain Freight Co.''

"Thanks for the warning,'' Harding said. "And now we'll be moving along. I don't imagine your visitors Dobbs and Faraday will give you any more trouble today.''

"Nope,'' Gagan said. "But tomorrow—that's a different story.''

When the two friends had put a hundred yards between themselves and the slower moving wagon, Harding said mildly, "I suppose you caught the name of the outfit he's working for, Feeney Freight Lines. That's us, in case you've forgotten.''

"I remember, all right,'' Frisco said. "It sounded like a good proposition, back there in Tragedy Springs. Dammit, I could kick myself for introducing you to Feeney.''

"Don't take it too hard,'' Allan counseled. "We've been up against tough odds before.''

"Oh, you'll probably figure some way out of it,'' Frisco grumbled. "Provided we don't get ourselves bushwhacked, and I don't freeze. Man, I never knew any place could be so cold.''

"Remember, we're nine or ten thousand feet above sea level,'' Harding reminded him. "But this is only September; wait till it really cools off.'' He grinned. "Anyway, it'll probably be warmer in Leadville, inside a cozy saloon.''

"It'll be warmer, all right,'' Frisco conceded. "In fact, if what the driver said about our competition is right, for us it'll likely be hotter than hell.''

Chapter Two

The Rocky Mountain Freight Company's office was situated on Leadville's crooked main street, near the south end of the business section. At about the time Harding and Noonan rode into town from the north, Moose Durham was listening to the report of his two employees.

"The bastard didn't give us no warning," Dobbs complained. "First thing we knew, he was shooting at us."

"I doubt that," Moose Durham said. "If he was as close as you say, he wouldn't have missed. Sounds to me like he aimed to throw a scare into you, and it looks as if he succeeded. I thought you had more guts than to be chased off so easily."

Dobbs cursed. "We ain't short on guts, dammit. How was we to know he wasn't a U.S. Marshal or something? Ain't that right, Faraday?"

The other one, short and thick, as contrasted with Dobbs, who was built like a bean pole, nodded agreement.

"That's why we didn't hang around, boss. Hell, if we'd been sure it wasn't the law, we would've handled it then and there."

Moose Durham, although he knew they were lying, decided not to make an issue of it. He gestured impatiently, and said, "What's done is done. The unfortunate thing is that you let the Feeney bring another load of supplies into Leadville. Next time I send you out to do a job, make sure it's done right. Savvy?"

"Sure, boss," Dobbs said, and Faraday nodded. The two of them left the office hurriedly, glad to be let off so easy. Outside, Dobbs said crossly, "It's easy for him to talk; he wasn't looking at the business end of a carbine."

"You should have mentioned that to him," Faraday said sarcastically. "He probably would have given you a raise. Right out the door on the toe of his boot."

Dobbs scowled at him, but didn't answer. He was a dull sort of person, more muscle than brains. Whenever he tried to match wits with Faraday, he came out second best. Besides, he wasn't in the best of shape, being cold and disgruntled. As usual when he felt that way, he headed for the Ace of Spades saloon. He didn't speak again until his belly had been warmed by two quick shots of whiskey. Feeling that he must justify himself somehow, he said threateningly, "If I see them two again, and if they ain't lawmen, I'll take 'em down a notch."

"Sure you will," Faraday agreed, having learned from experience that it was dangerous to contradict Dobbs when he had been drinking. "But it's likely you'll never get your chance. If Spud Gagan told them who we work for, they'll probably be smart enough to keep out of our way."

"That's another thing," Dobbs said. "I'm going to take care of Gagan, too. He didn't pay no attention when I told him to get off that wagon seat. Next time we won't give him a choice. It'll be into the canyon for him and the wagon both."

"And the horses?" Faraday inquired. "Them, too?"

Dobbs shook his head. "The boss would raise hell. He'll need the horses to pull his own wagons after he takes over Feeney's outfit." He signaled for the bartender to refill his glass.

"Speaking of Feeney," Faraday said. "I wonder where he is. I ain't seen him for a month."

"Somebody told me he went to a place called Tragedy Springs, over on the other side of the Divide," Dobbs said. "A funeral, or something. It wouldn't hurt my feelings none if he never came back. I wouldn't mind knocking that uppity female helper of his off her high horse." He grinned, showing tobacco-stained teeth. "Or doing something else to her, if you get what I mean." He touched a hand to the partially healed scar on his left cheek. "She gave me this with her buggy whip. Dammit, a woman's got no business running a freight line, not even while the owner's away."

Faraday, still being prudent, didn't answer, but devoted himself to his drink. He didn't share Dobbs' dislike for Molly Root, in fact he secretly admired her for her courage. There were very few evil things Faraday hadn't done, but he had never molested a decent woman. He didn't intend to start now. Not if he could help it. To change the subject, he said, "Soon as you get warm, we'd better mosey over to the yard. Ike's probably wondering what happened to us."

Dobbs muttered something, finished his drink, and the two of them left the saloon. They didn't pay for their drinks, knowing that the bartender would put them on Moose Durham's tab. That was one advantage of working for Durham; he believed in keeping his help happy. Unless they disobeyed his orders, in which case he might have you beat up or even killed.

The "yard" to which Faraday had referred was really a huge barn where Durham's six wagons and thirty or so horses could be sheltered from the weather. It was under the watchful eyes of Ike Langhorn, a man of middle age who had lost a leg on a bank job, and who always carried a chip on his shoulder. Since he was lightning fast with a sixgun, no one with good sense would risk making him angry, not even Dobbs. Langhorn took orders from Moose Durham, and from no one else.

When Dobbs and Faraday entered the barn there were only two wagons inside, and several of the stalls were empty. Three of the wagons were en route to or from Central City, the nearest point on the railroad. The other missing wagon was unloading supplies at one of the mines. Langhorn came stumping out of his cubbyhole office and looked at the two men balefully.

"You should have been here an hour ago. Someone saw you ride into town, and told me about it. Where've you been?"

When Dobbs hesitated, Faraday said, "We went to the office and talked with Moose Durham."

"Is that why you smell like whiskey?" Ike Langhorn demanded. "Since when has the boss been serving free drinks at the office?"

"Well, we stopped at the Ace of Spades," Faraday confessed. "We needed something to thaw us out."

"I'll give you something to warm you up," Langhorn said. "You see those empty stalls? They all need cleaning, and to have fresh straw put in. If that doesn't take the chill off, you can curry the horses."

Dobbs bristled, but before he could say anything, Faraday took him by the arm and turned him away. Langhorn went back into his cubbyhole, and Faraday said under his breath, "Let's not get him riled any more than he is. With his temper, he's liable to do most anything."

"But dammit, we ain't being paid to clean out stalls. Our job is to put the fear of God into Moose Durham's competition."

"Which we didn't do too well today," Faraday said pointedly. "We'd better take it easy until Moose has

12

time to cool off. Him and Ike Langhorn both. Besides, it really will warm us up."

"I'm warm enough as it is," Dobbs growled, but he followed Faraday to the stalls.

Chapter Three

When Dobbs and Faraday left Moose Durham's office, Allan Harding and Frisco Noonan were bellied up to the bar in the Fast Buck, a saloon at the north end of the main street. It was almost uncomfortably warm in there, after having been out in the cold so long, and Harding took off his fleece-lined longcoat. He was wearing a good-looking dark suit, and might have passed as a prosperous businessman except for his tied down holster.

Even Frisco thawed out enough to unbuckle his heavy coat, although he didn't take it off. His clothing, in contrast to Harding's, looked as though it might have been picked out of a ragbag. Like his companion, he was wearing a holstered gun slung low at his hip. After disposing of two quick shots of whiskey, he warmed up enough to speak.

"This liquor is pretty bad, but it sure starts your blood circulating. I was beginning to feel like that old biddy in the Bible, the one that turned to a pillar of ice."

Harding looked at him in surprise. "I never figured you to be a Bible student, Frisco."

"Aw hell, I sparked a girl once, when I was young and foolish, and she dragged me to a church meeting. It wasn't my idea. Afterwards, she up and married a whiskey salesman."

"That sounds reasonable," Harding said. "Compared to you, a whiskey peddler would be a fine

14

catch. Incidentally, it was a pillar of salt, not ice."

"Well, whatever," Frisco said. "Anyway, that's water over the dam." He glanced around to make sure they weren't being overheard, and added, "Now that we're here, what do we do, just walk into this Feeney place and tell them you're the new owner?"

"*We're* the owners, not just me," Harding corrected. "And to answer your question, I've been thinking it might be a good idea to get the lay of the land before we let anyone know why we're here. Nobody knows us, and for the time being we'll keep it that way. Are you warmed up enough to go outside again?"

"I'll never be warm," Frisco grumbled. "But I'm as near ready as I'll ever be."

"Good." Harding laid two dollars on the bar and pocketed his change. The bartender, a fat, shiny-pated man, looked at him speculatively.

"You gents planning to be around for a while?"

"We might," Allan said. "Any particular reason for asking?"

"Well, my old lady runs a boarding house, in case you're looking for somewhere to stay. Unless you're fixin' to put up at the hotel, that is. I'm not trying to take any business away from Moose Durham."

"Who's Moose Durham?" Harding asked.

"It's easy to tell you ain't been here before," the bartender said. "Moose Durham owns a piece of the hotel, like half the other places in town. He also owns the Rocky Mountain Freighting Company, and there's a rumor that he's got a slice of the Dead Indian mine."

"Sounds like he's a pretty important person," Harding commented. "I'll tell you what we'll do. We'll look the town over, including the hotel, and if we're interested in your wife's boarding house, we'll come back and get directions. By the way, we passed a freight

15

wagon as we came in, and I don't believe the name on it had anything to do with Rocky Mountain. Is there another freighting outfit in Leadville?"

"Yes and no," the bartender said. "A feller by the name of Feeney had a pretty good business until just recently, but I understand he's about to go under. Been having a lot of bad luck lately. Wagons hijacked, and one driver killed in a wreck. Feeney himself ain't been around for a few weeks. My guess is that he's off somewhere trying to unload his company on some poor sucker. Excuse me, I've got a customer."

Outside, Frisco said drily, "How do you like being called a poor sucker?"

"I've been called worse," Harding said with a grin. "But I admit our future doesn't look too bright. Let's get these horses stabled, and then we'll look over the town."

The two men climbed into their cold saddles. As they came to a curve in the street they could see that Leadville was more of a town than it had first appeared to be. Judging from the number of wagons on the road, and horses tied at the rails, the place was prospering.

Among other businesses which came into sight were an assay office, a general store, saddle shop, hardware store, two more saloons, and the hotel, a two-story frame structure, whose sign announced that it also served meals. Beyond the hotel, and separated from it by a vacant lot, was a sizable building bearing the sign FEENEY FREIGHT LINES. Almost directly across from this, on the opposite side of the street, was a small brick building with the wording ROCKY MOUNTAIN FREIGHTING CO. on the window.

"There's the livery barn," Frisco said, pointing past the Feeney building.

Most of the stalls in the livery stable were already in use, but the proprietor, a short, stout man who volunteered the information that his name was Abe Wilkins, said that he could take care of two more horses. "I'll unsaddle 'em and rub 'em down," he said. "The charge is a dollar fifty a night, or cheaper by the week, if you're planning to stay that long."

The price seemed a little high, but Harding handed him three dollars, saying as he did so, "We'll decide later if we want to pay by the week, Okay?"

Wilkins nodded, and Harding, after unfastening his saddlebags and putting them across his arm, headed for the street, followed by Frisco Noonan, who was swinging his arms in an effort to keep warm.

"If you ask me," Frisco muttered. "We'd be smart to get anything we can for what's left of the company, and head for Arizona, or someplace else that's warm. Maybe that other freighting company would buy us out."

"Don't be in such a rush," Harding said. "In the first place, we don't know what there is to sell, and in the second place, I wouldn't do business with an outfit that waylays its competitor's wagons."

"Besides which you're too danged stubborn to say quit," Frisco said. "I ought to know by now that you never dodge a fight."

"You're not exactly a dove of peace yourself," Harding said, smiling. "I've seen you in action once or twice."

By then they were passing the Feeney barn. One of the front corners had been made into an office, and through the window, Harding saw a woman seated at a desk. Her back was toward him, so he couldn't tell much about her.

"We'll look at the hotel first, and then find some

excuse to come back and see our pig-in-a-poke. Remember, we're not going to let anyone know we're the new owners. Not yet.''

They were almost to the hotel when a man's voice, coming from behind them, called, "Mr. Harding?"

Startled, and wishing his coat were still unbuckled so that he could get at his gun, Allan came to a stop and turned to look back. With relief, he saw that it was the man who had been driving the Feeney wagon, and who was now gesturing to him from in front of the barn. Allan turned and retraced his steps, Frisco alongside him.

"You made good time, Gagan," Allan said. "We can't have been in town over an hour."

"It was mostly downhill from where you last saw me," Gagan said. "I was just telling the boss what you did. Have you got time to come in for a minute?"

"The boss?" Harding echoed. "Some bartender told us Mr. Feeney was out of town. Sure, we're in no hurry."

Gagan turned and went back into the barn, with Harding and Frisco at his heels. He opened a door into the office cubicle, and said, "These are the two gents I was telling you about, boss. Harding and Noonan."

To Allan's surprise, there was no one else in the room except the woman. Seen at close range, she was younger and prettier, even though her dark hair was drawn into an unstylish knot at the back of her head, and she was wearing a faded brush jacket above men's Levi's.

"You're the boss?" Harding asked. "I thought Mr. Feeney . . ."

"You thought right," the girl cut in. "Spud Gagan is the only one who calls me 'boss.' It's just our little joke. By the way, I'm Molly Root. I work for Mr. Feeney. When he's away, I'm more or less in charge. I expect

18

him back soon."

Harding had an idea that the last was wishful thinking, but he didn't comment. For the first time, Molly Root smiled.

"Mr. Gagan was just telling me what you did for him out on the road. On behalf of Mr. Feeney and all of us, I thank you."

"You're welcome," Harding said. "Actually, we didn't do much, just stirred up a little dust. I notice you said 'all of us.' Do you have a big crew?"

Molly Root managed to look embarrassed and defensive at the same time.

"That was only an expression. Actually, there's just Mr. Gagan and me, and of course Mr. Feeney when he gets back. One of our drivers was killed recently, and the other one quit."

"Sorry to hear it," Harding said. "How did it happen?"

"His wagon was caught in a rockslide," she said flatly. "But what I can't understand . . ." Suddenly she frowned, and changed the subject.

"You aren't interested in hearing about our problems. Thanks again for what you did. I hope you enjoy your visit to Leadville."

This was too much for Frisco, who said sourly, "I'd like to know how anyone could enjoy freezing his ears off. Whose idea was it putting a town up here on the top of nowhere?"

"You could blame it on whoever put silver and lead in the ground," Molly said. "Some folks might say that was God."

"Sounds more like something the devil would think up," Frisco snorted. "You can have my share of it."

"I take it you don't approve of our climate," Molly Root said, smiling. "So you must have had some other

19

reason for coming here."

When Frisco fumbled for an answer, Harding said smoothly, "Just seeing the country, Mrs. Root. I've heard a lot about Leadville, and always wanted to look at it for myself."

"It's 'miss,' not 'missus,' " Molly Root said, and added unexpectedly, "Would you happen to be interested in a job? We could use another driver?"

Allan, caught off guard, said awkwardly, "The two of us stick together, Miss Root. Thanks just the same."

"We also need someone to ride shotgun," Molly said. "You see, I'm not sure it was really an accident that killed our driver. And you saw what happened out on the road today. I'll hire both of you, if you feel like going to work. You might as well know, though, that the jobs don't carry any guarantee. By this time next month, we may be out of business. Especially," she added grimly, "if Moose Durham has his way."

"Suppose you give us time to think it over," Harding suggested. "We just hit town an hour or so ago. Haven't even got us a room for the night yet."

"I didn't mean to rush you," Molly said. "About that room, if you don't mind a little advice, don't go to the hotel. It belongs to Moose Durham, and he'd know every move you make."

"Does this Durham live in the hotel?" Harding asked.

"Goodness no! He has a fine house where he lives with his sick wife and a housekeeper. But the man who runs the hotel would be spying on you, and after the run-in you had with Durham's men, that might not be so good. Besides which, the hotel is cold and drafty. There's a boarding house I can recommend. It's run by a Mrs. Cook, and she lives up to her name."

"Maybe we've heard of her," Harding said. "Is her

husband a bartender?''

"That's the one," Molly said. "I can point out her house to you from the window."

Afterwards, trudging toward the boarding house, Frisco said crossly, "You win the cigar, boy. You ain't really figuring to work for that female, are you? Hell's bells! We'd be working for ourselves. You know danged well Feeney ain't coming back."

"It might be interesting," Allan said. "And any time we want to, we can take over. What do you say?"

"Oh, I'll string along like always," Frisco said. "Damn it to hell, on top of everything else, it's beginning to snow."

Chapter Four

The boarding house was made of rock, and built on the side of a hill, so that it was two stories high in front, and only one at the back. Harding's knock was answered by a cheerful looking, rather stout little woman wearing a white apron over a woolen dress. After a quick visual appraisal, she opened the door wide and motioned them in.

"Don't stand there in the cold. Come inside where you can thaw out."

This was obviously all right with Frisco, who said, "Those are the first kind words I've heard today, ma'am. You'll get no argument from me." He followed Harding into the front hall, and quickly closed the door behind him.

"Mrs. Cook?" Harding inquired.

"That's me," she acknowledged, "although I'm known mostly as Hetty. You must be the two strangers that just rode into town."

"Now how did you know that?" Harding asked.

Hetty Cook smiled. "Nothing much happens around here that I don't find out about. I just came from the general store, and Angus McNab, he's the owner, mentioned seeing you ride by. Is it room and board you'd be wanting?"

"That's right," Harding said, and added with a grin, "You wouldn't be Irish now, would you?"

"As Irish as Paddy's pig," Hetty said, chuckling. "Before I became Mrs. Cook I was Henrietta

O'Sullivan. But about room and board, if you don't mind sharing the same bed, I can fix you up. There's just one room vacant at the moment. Would you like to see it?''

"I'm sure it will be fine," Harding said. "And since we're used to doubling up, that'll be no problem. Do you serve three meals a day?"

"Just breakfast and supper," Hetty said. "But I can make up some sandwiches or something at noontime if you want me to. And speaking of food, are you hungry right now?"

"We could do with a little nourishment," Harding conceded. "It's been a good while since breakfast."

"Then you tote your saddlebags up and look at the room. It's on the back, over to the left. I was about to have a bite myself, and I'll see if I can't scrape up enough for the three of us." She looked at Allan curiously. "Aren't you going to ask how much I charge?"

"We'll leave that up to you," Harding said. "To tell the truth, I doubt if I could drag Frisco out of here if I tried. By the way, we haven't introduced ourselves. I'm Allan Harding, and this handsome rascal is Frisco Noonan. We'll go look at the room and wash our hands."

The bedroom was small, but there was enough space for a dresser and a sizable double bed whose springs, as Harding found out, didn't sag. While he was making this discovery, Frisco crossed over to look out the window.

"Man, that snow is really coming down! I'm glad we're here instead of at the hotel, if it's as drafty there as the girl said."

"Is it the draft you're worrying about?" Harding asked, "Or did you notice the good smell coming out of

23

our landlady's kitchen? In either case, I agree with you. We're lucky she had a room left. And I'm glad it's at the back, with the window close to the ground. We just might want to get out that way sometime."

"Yeah? How come?"

"Well, after what happened out on the road, somebody might come gunning for us. Especially if we take those jobs Molly Root offered."

"We didn't promise her anything," Frisco said. "I still think we'd be smart to show her our bill of sale, sell out for whatever we can get, and hightail it out of here."

"You're forgetting something," Harding reminded him. "We traded Feeney a first-class saloon for this freighting business. It looks like we got stung, but I'm not going to write it off. Not yet, anyway."

"Well, I'll go along with you like always," Frisco said. "Between you and me and the gatepost, though, is it the money you're thinking about, or did you fall for Molly Root?"

"Don't talk crazy!" Harding said. "She's just a child. But speaking of money, we'd better find a safer place than your moneybelt for the cash we're carrying."

"Like a bank?" Frisco suggested. "That's where you put it back in Tragedy Springs."

"For one thing, I didn't notice any bank on the main street," Harding said. "And if there is one, I'm afraid our friend Moose Durham might own it, from what we've heard about him. I think I'll just ask our landlady to take care of it for us."

"Ain't that pretty risky? We've only known her fifteen minutes."

"Sometimes fifteen minutes is enough," Harding said. "However, the money's as much yours as it is mine. Have you got a better idea?"

Frisco scratched the stubble on his chin for a moment, then shook his head.

"She looks honest to me. Go ahead and ask her if you want to."

What Hetty "scraped up" turned out to be a full-fledged dinner, topped off with hot apple pie. She apologized for making them eat in the kitchen, saying that the dining room was already set for supper. Actually, the kitchen was very cozy, and after his heavy meal, Harding could hardly keep his eyes open. Frisco was even sleepier, and Harding said, "You fed us too well, Mrs. Cook. We'd better get out of here before we doze off."

"Call me Hetty," Mrs. Cook said. "And if you're sleepy, why don't you go up to your room and take a snooze? I'll call you in time for supper."

"Sounds like a good idea," Harding said, and shook Frisco by the shoulder.

"Come on, partner, and let the lady have room to work."

Frisco offered no resistance, and inside minutes was sound asleep on the bed. Harding grinned down at him, crossed over to the window, and looked out. He couldn't see much on account of the falling snow, and was tempted to follow Frisco's example, but restlessness made him decide to bundle up and go out. Molly Root would be wondering whether or not she had two new employees. He mght as well go over and put her mind at rest. Besides, despite what he had said to Frisco, he enjoyed the idea of seeing her again.

Harding bulled his way through the snow to the Feeney barn. No one was in the barn itself, although the two horses which had pulled Gagan's wagon were in their stalls. The wagon, still loaded, was sitting near the back of the barn, alongside another one. He knocked at the office door, and a feminine voice called, "Who is it?"

"It's me, Allan Harding."

A chair scraped, and light footsteps tapped on the floor. There was the sound of a bolt being slid, and the door was pulled open. Harding came to an abrupt stop on the threshold.

"What's the gun for?"

"I wasn't sure of your voice," Molly Root said, lowering the heavy pistol. "I thought you might be Dobbs or Faraday, pulling a trick on me, and I didn't dare take a chance."

Slightly nettled, Allan said shortly, "Aren't you taking a chance as it is, leaving that load of freight where anyone can help himself?"

"What else could I do?" she demanded. "Spud hasn't slept for thirty hours, and there was no one else I could call on. If you're going to say I should have closed the big doors, forget it. Anyone could open those without half trying."

"How about getting some help from the law?" Harding asked. "Leadville must have a sheriff or something."

She waited for him to come in, bolted the door, and went back to her desk before answering. "We have a town marshal, Dave Banks. He's very good, too, when it comes to shooting mad dogs or jailing drunk miners on Saturday night. He has one drawback."

"Which is?"

She smiled thinly. "He goes blind and deaf when it comes to dealing with anybody who works for Moose Durham."

"You mean he's on Durham's payroll?"

"I've never seen any money change hands, but I'd say the answer was yes."

"Well I'll be damned!" Harding said. "Begging your pardon, miss, but in my opinion there's nothing lower than a crooked lawman."

"Where's your feisty little friend?" she asked, as though tired of the subject.

"He's asleep," Harding told her. "We took your advice and went to Hetty Cook's boarding house. She not only rented us a room, but fed us such a big meal we almost burst. I decided to let Frisco sleep it off. Not much point going out anyway, not in this snowstorm."

"Yet *you* come out, Mr. Harding. I don't think you did it just to tell me about your big dinner."

"You're right," Harding said. "I came to tell you that we've decided to take those jobs you offered us."

Her relief was evident, although she tried not to make it too obvious. "I'm glad. You'll be paid fifty dollars apiece per month, and you can go to work as soon as the storm lets up. The first thing I want you to do is finish delivering that load of supplies. They go to the Rainbow mine. Your friend can drive, and you can ride shotgun. Then you can go up to Central City for another load. I want you to . . ."

"Whoa!" Harding said, holding up his hands. "There's one thing we'd better get straight right now. We'll work for you, but we'll do it our way, not yours. Just tell us what you want taken where, and let us figure out how to go about it."

Her face flushed, and she thrust out her chin defiantly. "You're like the rest of them, don't like taking orders from a woman. Why didn't you say so in the first place?"

"Because it isn't true," Harding told her. "You know something, miss? You really look good when you get mad. The point is, we'll do our best to keep the Feeney Freight Lines going, but we'll have to be allowed to use our own judgment. I don't think you'll be sorry."

"I already am," Molly said. "Sorry about a lot of things. Okay, you win. I'll tell you what goes where, and you figure out how to do it. But give me credit for having a little common sense. Remember, I've been here thee years, whereas you just rode in today. And never mind the compliments. So far as you're concerned, I'm just another man."

"Yes'm," Harding said. "I'll keep that in mind." Which, he added to himself, wouldn't be easy.

"Then that's settled," Molly said. "Will you start tomorrow?"

"I've already started," Harding said. "And the first thing I'm going to do is fix that big door so it won't be so easy to open." He slid back the bolt and stepped out into the barn. "You be sure to lock this again, and don't open it till you know who's out here."

"Oh Lord!" she exploded. "One minute on the job, and already *you're* giving orders to *me*!"

Chapter Five

Both Harding and Frisco were still too full to want any supper, so they went to bed without having met any of the other boarders. During the night the storm blew itself out. Harding, always an early riser, slid out from between the blankets and looked out the window. There wasn't as much snow as he had anticipated, only about three inches on the level. Apparently there had been more wind than snow, judging from the deep drifts piled up against the outbuildings. Shivering, he pulled on his pants and boots, then poured icy water from a granite pitcher into a washbowl and shaved, to the accompaniment of Frisco's contented snoring.

Nothing had been said about the time for breakfast, but when Harding opened the door into the hallway he could smell coffee. He closed the door, went back to the bed, and shook Frisco by the shoulder.

"Rise and shine, partner, unless you want to miss your breakfast."

Frisco was instantly awake and alert, the result of long habit. He swung his legs off the bed, winced as his bare feet touched the cold floor, and hurriedly put on his socks. Since he shaved only on Sundays, and today was Wednesday, he was dressed and ready in five minutes. The two of them went downstairs, and Hetty Cook came out of the kitchen to greet them.

"Food'll be ready in ten minutes, boys. Meanwhile the coffee is hot if you want some. Did you sleep all right?"

"Just fine," Harding said, as Frisco nodded.

"Coffee would hit the spot right now. Should we go in the dining room?"

"Yes. Mr. Guillford is already there. Go in and introduce yourselves. I've got things on the stove to watch."

Guillford proved to be a lanky, dour-looking man of around forty, dressed in town clothes. Some of his dourness left him as he stood up to shake hands. Smiling, he looked considerably younger.

"I'm Stacy Guillford. You must be the two who just moved in. Hetty was telling me about you."

"That's right," Allan said, gripping the man's outstretched hand. "I'm Allan Harding, and this is my friend and partner Frisco Noonan."

Guillford shook Frisco's hand in turn, and said, "Glad to meet both of you. You picked a rather bad day to arrive in Leadville. It isn't always like this; sometimes it's worse."

Frisco looked at him quizzically. "You mean it gets colder than it was yesterday?"

"Much colder," Guillford said. "And last night's snow was just a trace, compared to what we'll have later. Of course there's one good thing about the snow. In this thin air, it soon disappears. We don't usually have slush afterwards."

All three men sat down, and Harding took a sip of coffee, which was strong and hot. He could detect other appetizing aromas coming from the kitchen, and suddenly realized that he was exceedingly hungry. From the way Frisco was eyeing the kitchen door, Allan knew that he wasn't the only one who felt that way. To be polite, he asked Guillford, "What line of business are you in, Mr. Guillford?"

"I was hoping you'd get around to that," Guillford said, smiling. "In another minute I would have told you without being asked. I publish the local weekly newspaper. That's weekly with two 'e's.''

Frisco looked puzzled, but Harding smiled.

"What do you call your paper, Mr. Guillford?"

"The *Leadville Courier*," Guillford said. "And now that you know what I do, you won't think I'm just being nosy if I ask you a few questions. I want items for the newspaper. For instance I'd like to be able to tell my readers where you're from, what brought you to Leadville, and how long you intend to stay."

Harding grinned. "The answers, in that order are: Central City, our horses, and undecided."

Guillford spread his palms in mock despair.

"All right, be mysterious. But don't be surprised if I invent a few details. After all, I have to satisfy my subscribers. All four of them. And I have ways of finding things out. For instance I know you repaired the door to Feeney's barn."

"How did you discover that?" Harding asked.

"Very simply," Guillford said. "I saw you doing it. Unless you tell me to the contrary, I'll assume that you're working for Feeney Freight Lines."

The conversation was interrupted as Hetty Cook came into the room carrying a big plate of ham and eggs, which she placed on the table.

"You boys help yourselves. There'll be flapjacks in a few minutes. Take as much of everything as you want, but don't leave anything on your plates. At the prices Angus McNab charges, I can't stand to throw anything away."

"Not much danger of that," Harding said. "Not with my friend Frisco present. He's liable to eat the plate too."

Mrs. Cook laughed and went back into the kitchen. For a few minutes all three men were busy with their breakfasts. Harding was thinking about what Guillford

31

had just said. It might not be a bad idea to get a little publicity. He looked across the table.

"All right, Mr. Guillford, you can say in the *Courier* that we will be working for the Feeney Company. It will be pretty obvious anyway, when folks see us driving one of Feeney's wagons."

"You're a freighter? Somehow, you don't look the part."

"I've been a lot of things," Harding told him. "If working for Feeney makes me a freighter, so be it. And since you know what we'll be doing, you might also mention that the Feeney company contemplates expanding its operations. Or at least that's the impression I got when talking with Miss Root."

"Now we're getting somewhere," Guillford said enthusiastically. "Can you give me any further details?"

Harding smiled. "You wouldn't want to tell it all in one issue, would you? Save something for next week."

"That makes sense," Guillford said. "And now if you'll excuse me, I'll be on my way. The paper comes out on Friday." He got as far as the doorway into the hall, and turned around. "I suppose you realize that this is going to make at least one person unhappy, Moose Durham, owner of the Rocky Mountain Freight Co. He doesn't like competition."

"That's his problem," Harding said, as he forked a couple more flapjacks onto his plate.

Frisco waited for the front door to open and close, then said curiously, "How come you gave him that hogwash about expanding? You know it ain't so."

"Do I?" Harding asked, grinning. "The company hired two men yesterday, you and me. Couldn't you call that expanding?"

"Whatever you call it," Frisco said, "You're going to

make somebody sore. And I ain't talking about that man Durham. Molly Root will likely chew your head off."

"I wouldn't be surprised." Harding agreed. "So let's go down and give her a chance. If you've finished stuffing yourself, that is."

Outside, the sunshine on the fresh snow was almost blinding. Not so blinding, however, as to keep the two men, when they approached the Feeney barn, from noticing that one pane of the office window had been shattered, and was covered on the inside by a piece of cardboard. As they entered the office, Molly Root, seated at her desk, looked grim. Without so much as a good morning, she said furiously, "Look what someone did to that window during the night."

"Are you sure it wasn't the wind?" Harding asked.

She picked up a fist-sized rock. "The wind didn't blow this through the glass. I found it in the middle of the floor."

Harding held out his hand for the rock. "Has anything like this ever happened before?"

Molly shook her head, and Harding turned to look at Frisco, who was scowling. "How about it, partner, wouldn't you say this had something to do with what happened out on the road yesterday?"

"I sure as . . . I sure would," Frisco said. "Those two jaspers must've done it to get back at us. Dammit, why couldn't they face us man to man?"

Before answering, Harding moved over to the window and peered across at the brick office opposite. He thought he detected movement behind the window. Over his shoulder, he said, "I've got a hunch that Dobbs and Faraday weren't acting on their own. I think I'll go across the street and have a little talk with friend Durham."

"Oh no!" Molly exclaimed. "If you make him mad, there's no telling what he'll do."

Harding turned to look at her. "There's no reason for him to get mad when I just return something one of his employees mislaid. It's only common courtesy."

"That's crazy," Molly said. "And you know it."

"And how would *you* handle it," Harding asked. "Just roll over and play dead, as if it had never happened?"

Molly didn't answer, but her eyes flashed. Harding grinned.

"I didn't think you would, miss. You don't strike me as a quitter. Frisco will stay here, in case they try something else, and I'll go pay Durham a social call." He left the office, went out through the big doorway, and crossed the street.

Moose Durham had evidently been watching through the window, for he showed no surprise when Harding entered his office. A big man, but not fat, he looked up at Harding coldly.

"Folks generally knock before they come in. Now that you're here, who are you and what do you want? Also, what are you planning to do with that rock?"

Harding smiled. "I imagine you already know who I am, Mr. Durham. You've certainly been watching me closely enough through the window. Incidentally, you can shut your desk drawer. You won't be needing a gun. I'm here on a peaceful mission." He stepped up and laid the rock on Durham's desk. "One of your hired hands mislaid this and may be looking for it. It was probably either Dobbs or Faraday."

"I don't know what you're talking about," Durham said.

"That's strange," Harding said. "I've been told that you're pretty well up on whatever goes on here in Leadville. You disappoint me."

Durham flushed with anger, but his voice was under control. "I'm not interested in your opinions, Harding. I don't—"

"Oh? So you do know me, after all. You were about to say?"

"I was going to say that I don't have to listen to your wild rambling. On second thought, I'd like to know exactly what you're getting at."

"Just this," Harding said. "My friend and I are working for the Feeney Freight Lines now. When you return this rock to its previous owners, tell them that the next time they interfere with a Feeney wagon, I won't aim to miss."

"Why damn you!" Durham exploded. "You can't talk to me like that!"

"I just did," Harding said complacently. "One more thing, remind your men that anyone can throw rocks. It would be a shame if something happened to your nice big window." He backed to the door, stopping to add, "By the way, don't fail to read this week's *Courier*. Something in there may interest you."

Durham sat in stony silence as Harding left the office, carefully closing the door behind him.

Chapter Six

Harding returned to the Feeney office, and was reporting to Molly and Frisco on his conversation with Durham, when a young boy came in and said hesitantly, "Pa won't be coming to work today, ma'am. He's sick."

"I'm sorry," Molly said. She explained to the two men that this was Spud Gagan's oldest son, Tod. To the boy she added, "Is it anything serious? Maybe Dr. Mapes ought to see him."

Tod shook his head.

"Pa doesn't want the doctor. He says he'll be all right in a day or so. He said to tell you he's sorry, leaving you without a driver."

Molly laid a hand on his shoulder and said soothingly, "Tell him not to worry, just to take care of himself until he feels well enough to come back to work. And it might make him feel better to know that the two men he met on the road are working for us. He'll know the ones I mean. Thank you for bringing us the message."

"Yes'm," Tod said, and hurried away.

Harding looked at Molly. "Does Gagan do this often? Stay off sick, I mean?"

"Heavens no! He hasn't missed a day in the three years I've been here."

"I wonder . . ."

"Wonder what?" Molly inquired.

"Nothing. I just think I'll go have a look at him. Where does he live?"

Molly told him, and he glanced at Frisco.

"You might get that loaded wagon ready to take up to the mine. When I come back, we'll make the delivery."

Frisco nodded, and Harding left the office. He had no trouble locating Gagan's little house, and was admitted by Spud's wife, a neat, soft-spoken woman who was obviously trying to conceal her worry.

"I'm Allan Harding, ma'am. Could I speak with your husband a minute?"

"Oh, you're one of the men he was telling me about," she said, sounding relieved. "He doesn't want to see anyone, but since it's you, and if you won't stay long, I guess it'll be all right."

"I won't tire him," Harding promised, and Mrs. Gagan showed him into the bedroom.

Spud was in bed, and one look convinced Harding that his guess had been correct. The Feeney driver had taken a bad beating. One eye was swollen shut, and there were numerous cuts and bruises on his face. Despite this, he tried to grin.

"Guess I ain't very pretty, am I? For your information, I feel about half as good as I look."

Harding glanced over his shoulder to make sure that Mrs. Gagan had left the room. He asked grimly, "Dobbs and Faraday?" Gagan nodded.

"That's all I wanted to find out," Harding said. "Just take it easy. Frisco and I will keep things running. See you later."

Frisco had harnessed a team to the wagon by the time Harding got back. He looked up at Harding knowingly.

"He wasn't just plain sick, was he?"

"No. Dobbs and Faraday gave him a working over. I didn't get any details, but they did a good job of it."

"Yellow cowards," Frisco said harshly. "They seem

37

to favor odds of two to one. I reckon somebody ought to teach them a lesson."

"All in good time," Harding said. "Our first job is to deliver these supplies. By the way, I don't see any point in telling the girl what happened. Let her think Gagan's really sick."

"Sure," Frisco agreed. "You don't suppose they'd beat up a woman, do you?"

Harding shook his head. "I doubt if their boss Durham would stand for it. He doesn't want the whole town down on him. Folks can be pushed just so far. Did Molly happen to tell you where this Rainbow mine is located?"

"Nope. We didn't talk any more after you left."

"Well, I'll go find out. Then you can drive the wagon and I'll trail along on my horse. If anybody tries to make trouble, I want to be able to move fast."

Molly looked up from her work as Harding entered the office. "Is Spud Gagan very sick?"

"He's a long way from well, but it doesn't appear to be anything serious. Where's the Rainbow mine?"

Molly crossed to the window and pointed. "Take that road just beyond the livery stable. The mine is about nine miles west of town. You'll see the sign."

"Are we supposed to collect," Harding asked, and Molly nodded. She picked up a paper off her desk and handed it to him.

"Here's the bill. Mr. Gunderson is the man to see."

"Good. We're on our way."

As Molly had said, the mine wasn't hard to find. Harding and Frisco kept a sharp lookout, but no one tried to stop them. Frisco pulled the wagon to a stop at the mine storehouse, while Harding tied his sorrel at the office rail and went in. A small, red-faced man looked at him across the counter.

38

"Something I can do for you, stranger?"

"Mr. Gunderson?"

"That's right. Who are you?"

"Allan Harding, and I work for the Feeney Freight Lines." He shook hands with the red-faced man. "We've got a wagonload of supplies at your shed. Here's a bill for the hauling." He laid the paper on the counter. "I suppose you'd like to check the load before you pay for it."

"That won't be necessary," Gunderson said. "I've never had any trouble with the Feeney Company." He opened a drawer and counted out the money. "Is Mr. Feeney back yet?"

"No, and we don't expect him for a few days."

"Well, I'd rather tell him this to his face, but since he isn't here, I'll tell it to you. We'll be making other arrangements for our hauling from now on."

Harding looked at him in surprise.

"I don't understand, Mr. Gunderson. You just said you'd never had any trouble. We'll continue to give you good service, even while Mr. Feeney is away. Miss Root understands the office end of it, and we now have three drivers. What's your complaint?"

"No complaint, it's just a question of dollars and cents. We can have our freighting done at half the cost."

This could mean only one thing, Harding decided. Moose Durham was using this means of forcing the Feeney company out of business.

"I take it you're talking about the Rocky Mountain Freight Co. Right?"

Gunderson nodded, and Harding went on.

"Can't you see what Durham is up to? He intends to squeeze out the competition. What do you suppose will happen to his rates when he has the field to himself?"

39

"I've thought about that," Gunderson said. "But our stockholders would raise Ned if I paid more for hauling than I had to. Stockholders don't look far into the future. Damn it, I hate doing this, but there's no way out."

"Maybe there is," Harding said. "If the rates were the same, would you continue to use our wagons?"

"Of course. But like I told you . . ."

"We'll meet Durham's price," Harding said.

"No matter how low he goes?" Gunderson demanded.

"No matter how low he goes," Harding said. "Now can we continue to do your hauling?"

"Why, yes," Gunderson said. "But I don't understand how you can do it. Moose Durham is rich. He can outlast Feeney."

"Suppose you let us worry about that," Harding said, with more confidence than he felt. "Anything to keep your stockholders happy. Now if you'll excuse me, I'll go help my partner unload the supplies."

Frisco looked dubious when Harding told him what he had promised. "What are we going to use for money? From the looks of things, Feeney didn't leave much when he cleared out."

"You still have that cash in your moneybelt, don't you?"

"Hey! Wait a minute! You ain't fixin' to throw good money after bad! Not for another man's outfit."

Harding grinned. "You're forgetting something, partner. You and I *are* the Feeney company. Maybe nobody else knows it, but we do. We're going to fight Durham to the last ditch."

"And end up broke," Frisco said glumly. "Man, I've seen you do some wild things before, but this . . . say, how are you going to explain this to Molly Root? She

40

makes out the bills and handles the money."

"I haven't figured that out yet," Harding admitted. He thought it over for a minute, and added, "There's no two ways about it, we'll have to tell her we own the company. I reckon it will be quite a shock, but she isn't the sort to panic. And I think she'll go along with it. Come on, let's get back and find out."

The return trip was made without incident, and they found Molly in the office, putting a new pane of glass in the window. Noting their expressions, she said drily, "You needn't look so surprised. I'm not as helpless as you seem to think. I got the hardware store to cut the glass to size, and bought a dime's worth of putty. Did everything go all right?"

"Not exactly," Harding said. "Oh, we delivered the load, and got paid for it, but Mr. Gunderson told me we wouldn't be getting any more of their business."

"For heaven's sake why? He was one of our best customers."

"He still is," Harding said, smiling. "You see his only reason for quitting was that our friend across the street has lowered his rates. I told him we'd match anything Rocky Mountain offered."

"*You* told him? What right—"

"You'd better sit down," Harding said. "I'm afraid you're in for a shock."

"Another shock, you mean," Molly said, but she crossed to her desk and sat down. "You've already made a promise that we can't keep. What else did you do?"

Instead of answering directly, Harding took a piece of paper out of his pocket, unfolded it, and laid it in front of her on the desk. She read it twice, and looked up at him in disbelief.

"Is this real?"

41

"I'm afraid it is," Harding said. "Frisco and I were gullible enough to believe everything Feeney told us. We traded him a profitable saloon for a freighting company that was on its last legs."

"Oh Lord!" Molly groaned. "Why didn't you tell me this in the first place? Letting me make a fool of myself hiring you like a couple of drifters."

"We didn't mean it that way," Harding said. "But after our run-in with Dobbs and Faraday we decided to wait until we saw how things shaped up. Now it looks like we might as well come out in the open. If we've upset you, I'm sorry. And another thing, we'd appreciate it if you'd stay on the same as before. You know more than we do about the freighting business."

Somewhat appeased, Molly managed a smile. "I have no objections to working for you, but I don't foresee much future. Not if we operate at a loss. Even with the money you just collected, the business has only about two hundred dollars cash."

"We intend to invest some more capital," Harding said. "Right, Frisco?"

"That's what you keep telling me," Frisco grumbled. "Well, we've been busted before. What the hell . . . excuse me, miss. Money ain't everything."

"Then it's all settled," Harding said. "The next thing is to let Moose Durham know we aren't throwing in the towel."

Molly looked worried.

"You aren't going over there again, are you? This time he'll be ready for you."

Harding shook his head. "No, I don't intend to pay him another visit. He's not the only one I want to know about this. Is there anything we're supposed to be doing right now?"

"Not today," Molly said. "There'll be some supplies

at Central City Saturday for another one of the mines, but you won't have to leave until tomorrow. Where are you going?"

"To see Stacy Guillford," Harding said. "It may not be too late to get a notice in this week's *Courier*."

Chapter Seven

Harding was halfway to the *Courier* office when a buggy drew up alongside him, and a well remembered woman's voice called, "Hi there, stranger. What's your hurry?"

Surprised, Harding looked around at the driver of the buggy, and a broad smile lit up his face. "Mazie Bowen! I'll be a dirty son."

The woman who had accosted him was in her late forties, as Harding knew, but she appeared ten years younger, and she still retained much of her stunning good looks. Harding stepped off the board walk and moved out beside the buggy. Mazie smiled at him with undisguised pleasure, and said in a rather throaty voice, "Get in the buggy, and I'll give you a lift. Unless you're afraid of ruining your reputation by being seen with me, that is."

Harding grinned as he stepped up into the buggy. "If it ever comes to a choice between you and my reputation, I'll take you every time. How long has it been? Five years?"

"At least," Mazie said. "And don't tell me I haven't changed, because I know damned well that I have. Though not in such a way that the good ladies of the town will speak to me. Not that some of their husbands aren't glad enough to come up to my place when they think no one's looking."

"I take it you're still in the same line of business, then?"

"Sure. Why give up a good thing? I've got a pretty nice house on the edge of town, and three young ladies working for me." She placed special emphasis on the words "ladies." "Where are you headed, by the way?"

"Just to the newspaper office," Harding said.

"Too bad. I was hoping we could have a nice long ride." She jiggled the lines, and the buggy began to move. "I'd like to hear what you've been doing since we last met. Getting in and out of trouble, I bet. And I suppose you're still palling around with that ornery Frisco."

"He's not really ornery," Harding said. "He just tries to give folks that impression."

"I know," Mazie told him. "Between you and me, I've always liked the old buzzard. Tell him to drop around and see me. You're invited, too, although I know that in your case it'll be just a social visit. But tell me, what are you doing in Leadville?"

Harding shrugged. "Getting into trouble, as you just guessed, though heaven knows I didn't intend to. I'll tell you something, and I'd rather you'd keep it under your hat until it comes out in the paper. Frisco and I are the new owners of the Feeney Freight Lines."

"Oh Lordy!" Mazie exclaimed. "This time you're really asking for it. I presume you know about Moose Durham?"

"A little," Harding said. "And what I've heard doesn't sound good. But suppose you fill me in on the details. How come everyone around here jumps when you mention his name?"

"Everyone except me, that is," Mazie amended. "Well, maybe a few others, such as Molly Root." She looked at Harding obliquely. "Speaking of whom, as the schoolteacher would say, what do you think of Molly?"

"She's got a lot of savvy," Harding replied. "In fact I don't know how we'd get along without her. I have a hunch she knows more about the business than Feeney ever did. Although Feeney's no fool in some respects. He succeeded in swapping us a practically defunct freight line for a first-class saloon in Tragedy Springs."

"So that's how come you're in Leadville," Mazie said. "But let's get back to Molly Root. You haven't said anything about how pretty she is. Are you getting old, or is your eyesight failing?"

Harding grinned. "My eyes are all right, and I'm not *that* old, but I've got just enough sense not to go overboard for any woman, no matter how pretty she is. Besides, Molly is young enough to be my daughter. By the way, we just passed the *Courier*."

"I was hoping you wouldn't notice," Mazie said, pulling the rig to a stop. "But go on. Tell me why you shouldn't fall for a nice young lady. You're going to have to settle down sometime."

"Maybe so, but not for a few years yet. Say, what's going on here? Have you started giving advice to the lovelorn or something? Suppose we forget Molly Root, and you just answer my question. Why is everyone—I should say *almost* everyone—afraid of Moose Durham?"

"Well, for one thing, he's got a finger in just about every pie in town. If he wanted to foreclose on a few mortgages, he could put half the merchants out of business. On top of that, he has a bunch of roughnecks working for him, including a few who would just as soon shoot a man as not. Or get rid of him in some other way. I suppose you've heard about one of the Feeney wagons going off the road and killing the driver. Maybe you think that was an accident?"

"No," Harding said. "Because Frisco and I came

46

along just in time to prevent it happening again. This time to a driver named Gagan."

"Then you're already on Durham's black list," Mazie said, and reached over to touch his hand. "I know how stubborn you can be, but take the advice of an old friend and move on before it's too late. Please?"

Harding was impressed by her sincerity. He had never seen her so serious before. For a moment he was tempted to follow her advice. Then he shook his head.

"I appreciate what you're trying to do, and I'm obliged to you, but I can't cut and run. I'd always hate myself for it."

She sighed resignedly. "Well, it was worth a try. Don't say I didn't warn you."

"I won't," Harding promised. He started to get out of the buggy, then turned back.

"Is there anything else you can tell me about Moose Durham that I ought to know? I don't suppose he's a customer of yours."

"No, although most of his men are, which is why I'm so sure of what happened to that wagon. They're inclined to talk too much when they . . . anyhow, I suppose you know about his so-called housekeeper, Lola Marchant, as she calls herself now."

"I've never met her," Harding said. "But I've heard her mentioned. Also his sick wife."

"The part about Mrs. Durham being sick is on the level, although nobody, including Doc Mapes, seems to know what's the matter with her. But Lola . . ." She grimaced. "If that woman is a housekeeper, I'm Joan of Arc. She used to work at a house in Pueblo. Now she's in business for herself. It's no wonder Mrs. Durham is sick, living under the same roof with her husband's private . . . well, you get what I mean. But be careful of Lola. She can be as dangerous as Moose.

47

You're the first person in Leadville I've told this, but Lola, who wasn't using that name at the time, killed a man in Colorado City. Of course she got off scott free. Why wouldn't she, when half the men on the jury patronized her place of business, and were afraid of what she could tell? The jury foreman called it justice. I call it blackmail."

She looked at Harding and smiled wryly. "Naturally, if it was me on trial, instead of Lola, I'd look at it differently. They couldn't pick a jury around here without having a few men on it who'd be afraid of what I might reveal. Lord knows I wouldn't stand a chance with a woman jury, but thanks be it hasn't come to that yet. Although I understand that up in Wyoming Territory, the women . . . ." She broke off suddenly and made a self-deprecatory gesture.

"There I go again on my favorite subject, the stupidity of women. You didn't ask for a speech. Let's get back to you. What's your business with Mr. Guillford?"

"I'm placing a notice in the next issue of the *Courier*," Harding said. "About Frisco and me taking over the freight line."

Mazie chuckled, and Harding looked at her inquiringly.

"What's so funny?"

"Oh, I was just picturing the expression on Moose Durham's face when he sees your notice," Mazie said. She held out her hand. "It's been nice knowing you, Allan Harding. I'll see you at the funeral."

"Who's?" Harding asked. "Mine or Moose Durham's?"

"That depends on whether your luck holds out," Mazie said. "I've seen you in some pretty tight spots before, but this time you're really in it up to your ears.

48

Good luck.''

"Thanks," Harding said, and watched her drive off. He had the uncomfortable feeling that her advice had been good. Probably the smart thing would be to take his losses and run. As she had said, he hadn't a chance against Moose Durham and his bunch of hardcases. But dammit . . .

He turned and headed for the newspaper office.

Chapter Eight

The *Leadville Courier* office was situated in a back room behind the saddle shop. Stacy Guillford was setting type when Harding entered. He looked up, smiled, and said, "I'd offer to shake hands, but then you'd be as inky as I am. There's a chair under that pile of trash if you can find it."

"I'll stand," Harding said, glancing around. "Do you run this place by yourself?"

"You're looking at the whole crew," Guillford said. "Reporter, printer, editor, and even delivery boy. There's one advantage to this arrangement. I don't have any labor trouble. You won't mind if I keep on working? The paper comes out tomorrow."

'Go right ahead," Harding said. "But I hope I'm not too late to get something in this week's edition."

"Never too late for that," Guillford said. "Do you have a hot news item that'll sell extra copies?"

"Some folks might think it's hot. Moose Durham, for instance. In the first place, you can elaborate on that item about Frisco Noonan and me. We're the new owners of the Feeney Freight Lines."

"The devil you say! I *thought* you were holding out on me. Are there any more details?"

"Not for your gossip column," Harding said. "But I'd like to insert a notice, and pay for it."

Guillford wiped his hands on an inky cloth and moved up to a small counter. He picked up a pencil, and pulled a scratchpad toward him. "Okay, Mr. Harding, let's have it."

"Make it something like this," Harding said. "Noonan and Harding, the new owners of the Feeney Freight Lines, will continue to provide fast and efficient service as in the past. Rates will be adjusted to match those of any competitor. We solicit your business."

Guillford finished scribbling, and gave Harding a slanting look. "Competitor in this case of course meaning Moose Durham and his Rocky Mountain Freight Co. What are you planning to do, start a price war?"

"It's already been started," Harding said. "Not by us, by Durham. You can improve the wording if you want to, so long as the meaning stays the same."

The newspaper man rubbed his jaw reflectively. "I admire your spirit, Mr. Harding, but do you realize exactly what you're doing? My opinion of Durham isn't high, but he's a smart businessman. And he's well-heeled."

Harding smiled. "How do you know, or more important, how does Durham know that we're not well-heeled too? Maybe running the freight line is just a hobby with us. Anyway, go ahead and publish the notice. It doesn't have to be big. I'm fairly sure the right people will see it."

"Whatever you say," Guillford acquiesced. "I'll make it just one column wide. That'll be two bucks and a half." He grinned. "I really shouldn't charge you a cent. I've got a feeling this will generate a lot of news for future editions."

Harding paid him and left the print shop. Passing through the front room, he was spoken to by the Mexican saddlemaker, who said politely, "Excuse me, *señor*. I think maybe you like to know someone has been watching through the window. A man I have heard called Dobbs."

51

"Thanks," Harding said. "I'll see if I can catch up with him."

Dobbs was not on the street, but there was a saloon nearby into which he could have ducked, a place called the Mexicali. On impulse, Harding went in.

There were three Mexicans at the bar, which surprised him, as he hadn't expected to find many men of that nationality so far north. Except for those three, and a bartender who was also Mexican, the place was deserted. However there was a closed door near one end of the bar. A little recklessly, Harding crossed to the door, pushed it open, and almost knocked down Dobbs, who had evidently been listening. Dobbs made a move for his gun, saw that he could be outdrawn, and changed his mind. He said with a mixture of fear and bravado, "What's the idea, banging into me like that?"

"You shouldn't have had your ear glued to the door," Harding said. "I understand you've been looking for me. What's on your mind?"

Dobbs shook his head. "I ain't been looking for you. Whatever gave you that idea?"

"It isn't important," Harding said. "Anyway, I wanted to see you. Come out front, where the light's better."

When Dobbs didn't move, Harding grabbed him by the front of his jacket and yanked him through the doorway. The Mexicans, none of whom had said a word since Harding had entered, backed off as though sensing trouble. It was obvious that they were going to remain neutral. Apparently they considered this an issue between gringos.

"Where's your pal Faraday?" Harding asked. "I thought you worked as a team. Well, never mind, you can pass this along to him. A friend of mine was beaten up last night. Somebody poked him in the eye. Like this . . ." Harding landed a short jab on Dobb's left eye.

"Why damn you!" Dobbs snarled. He swung a haymaker which Harding easily ducked. However, Dobbs followed it with a low punch which made Harding gasp. Dobbs, for all his stringbean look, was certainly not lacking in muscle. Harding fell into a crouch, and rammed a fist into Dobbs's chest, almost knocking him down.

The bartender was yelling something in Mexican, probably telling them to take their fight outside, but Harding had more important things to think about. He landed a blow which opened a cut on Dobbs's cheek, and took one on the chin in return. His respect for Dobbs's fighting ability was increasing.

Unknown to Harding, one of the Mexicans had gone for help. The saloon door banged open, and a heavy voice said with authority, "Break it up, you two!"

Harding's back was to the door, but when Dobbs retreated, he risked a quick look over his shoulder. A big man was standing spread-legged, with one hand resting on a holstered sixgun. More important, there was a star pinned to his vest. This must be the lawman Molly Root had told him about. Harding decided to be prudent. He straightened up and let his hands fall to his sides.

"Marshal Banks?"

"That's right," the marshal said. "What's going on here?"

"Why, nothing at all, Marshal." Harding said innocently. "We were just horsing around." He turned to look at his adversary.

"Isn't that right, Dobbs?"

Dobbs hesitated a moment, then nodded. He probably didn't want trouble with the law any more than Harding did. Either that, or he didn't want Spud Gagan's beating brought into the light.

Harding thought the marshal looked relieved, and he remembered something Molly had said about Marshal Banks going blind and deaf when Moose Durham's men were involved. Still, the marshal had to make a show of authority. He said bluntly, "If neither of you has any complaint, I'll let it ride. But don't let it happen again. Understand?"

"Of course, Marshal," Harding said. He waited for Banks to leave the saloon, then returned his attention to Dobbs.

"Like the man said, we'll let it ride. For now, that is. But about that friend of mine, the one who was beaten up. If anything happens to him again, I'll take it personal. Do you get the idea?"

Dobbs nodded grudgingly, and Harding added, "You can tell that to Faraday, or anyone else you think may be interested. And by the way, the same goes for the Feeney place, in case you get the urge to throw any more rocks. Now get the hell out of here! I don't want you looking at my back as I leave."

"You ain't heard the last of this," Dobbs threatened, but he passed Harding and left the saloon. Harding stepped up to the bar and faced the bartender.

"Do you speak English?"

"*Si*. I mean, yes."

"Good, because my Mexican is pretty rusty. I apologize for causing a commotion. If you serve gringos, I'll take a shot of whiskey." He gestured toward the other patrons. "Set them up for these gentlemen, and one for yourself, too." He laid some money on the bar.

"*Gracias*," the bartender said. He showed perfect white teeth in a smile. "That Dobbs, I like to see him

54

bleed."

Harding returned the smile. "I didn't come off so well myself, but it was worth it." He glanced at the mirror behind the bar and added, "I'm going to have a sore jaw for a few days, but I talk too much anyway. *Adios*."

Returning to the Feeney office, Harding found Molly alone. She looked at him in dismay.

"What in the world happened to your chin? Didn't Mr. Guillford want to take your ad?"

"He was delighted," Harding said. "I had a little argument with our friend Dobbs. There's something I guess you ought to know. Gagan isn't sick; Dobbs and Faraday beat him up."

Molly didn't react as he had expected her to. She said matter-of-factly, "I suspected it was something like that. It didn't seem reasonable that Spud would get sick the first day after you and your friend had that trouble out on the road. I suppose you hunted up Dobbs to teach him a lesson?"

"Actually, he was following me," Harding said. "But I'll grant you I didn't try very hard to dodge him."

She gave an exasperated sigh.

"One day under new ownership, and you've cut out all our profit, excuse me, *your* profit; Spud Gagan has been beaten up; someone has thrown a rock through the window, and now you've had a brawl with one of Moose Durham's men. What are you tring to do? Start a war?"

"I'm trying to end one," Harding said. "But you're right, before this is over, it may get worse. If you want to quit, I've got no right to ask you to stay."

"Do I look like a quitter?" Molly demanded.

"No," Harding said, grinning. "I just wanted to give

55

you an out. I'm glad you didn't take it. How would you like to be a partner along with Frisco and me?"

"No, thank you," Molly said. "I couldn't contribute any capital, and I don't take charity."

"Have it your own way," Harding shrugged. "Where's Frisco, by the way?"

"Down at the livery stable. I told him, that is I suggested to him that you might as well keep your saddle horses here, since we've got room for them, and it will save money."

"Good idea. When he brings them back, I'm going to take a little ride. Frisco can stay in here, in case there's trouble."

"Do you think he could handle it?"

Harding laughed. "Frisco looks old and worn out, but you'd be surprised what he can handle. I'd hate to have him for an enemy."

"You know him better than I do," Molly said. "Where are you planning to ride, if it's any of my business."

"Everything we do is your business," Harding said. "To answer your question, I intend to ride a few miles on the road to Central City. We came over it yesterday, but I didn't pay much attention to details. Like good spots for an ambush, for instance. If Frisco and I are going out there tomorrow, I want to know what to expect. Not changing the subject, but where do you live?"

"At Hetty Cook's boarding house," Molly said, smiling. "Now you know why I could recommend it. Why do you ask?"

"I was afraid you might be living alone. I don't think Moose Durham would make war on a woman, but I feel a lot more confident knowing you're at Mrs. Cook's." He frowned. "How come I didn't see you at breakfast?"

"I ate early, in the kitchen. But there might be some disadvantages to our all living in the same place. If Dobbs and Faraday take a notion to burn the boarding house, we'll all go up together."

"I hadn't thought of it that way. Here comes Frisco now. I'll go take that ride. You can tell him the new developments."

"All right," she said. "And see if you can keep out of fights until we meet again. You don't want to miss one of Hetty's suppers."

Chapter Nine

Ike Langhorn tapped his peg leg on Moose Durham's office door, then entered without waiting for an invitation. He was the only one of Durham's men who could do that without arousing the boss's ire. His relationship with Durham went back many years, to the time when both of them had been small-time outlaws in Oklahoma. Now that he was crippled, Ike was relegated to the comparatively humble position of strawboss of the Rocky Mountain Freighting Company's barn. He secretly resented this minor post, but Durham paid him well, so he never complained outwardly, venting his discontent instead on those who were unfortunate enough to work under him.

Durham looked up from some waybills on his desk and asked, "Is something wrong at the barn?"

Langhorn shook his head. "Not in the way you mean. Dobbs just came in with a black eye and split cheek. He didn't want to talk about it, but I wormed it out of him that he was fighting with that new man, Harding, from across the street. The way Dobbs tells it, he got the best of it, but I have my doubts."

"So do I," Durham said. "I saw Harding through the window a few minutes ago, and he didn't seem to be in bad shape. What were they fighting about?"

"Harding found out that Dobbs and Faraday beat up on Spud Gagan."

Durham banged a big fist on the desk.

"The damn fools! They bungled the job I told them

to do, and then took it on themselves to work over Gagan. That was their idea, not mine. We won't run the Feeney company out of business by laying up one or two drivers for a day or so, not now that they have two new ones over there. How did Dobbs bump into Harding anyway?''

''It seems Dobbs saw him go through the saddle shop and into the newspaper office. Harding must have spotted him, either that or the saddlemaker tipped him off. Dobbs ducked into the Mex saloon, but Harding found him. That's where they fought. Oh yes, one of the customers went for Marshal Banks, and he broke it up.''

''Without arresting anybody?''

''That's right. He wouldn't have the nerve to throw one of your men in jail, and Dobbs didn't want Gagan's beating brought into the open, so he said they were just fooling around.''

''Well thank the Lord Dobbs had that much sense anyway. I wonder what Harding was doing at the print shop. He said something to me about being sure to read the *Courier* this week.''

''Harding was in here?'' Langhorn said in surprise.

''That's right. He brought this rock. Claims I had it thrown through Feeney's window. I suppose that was another of Dobbs's and Faraday's bright ideas.''

Langhorn debated with himself a moment before saying, ''Sometimes I wonder why you keep those two around.''

Durham was slow in answering, and Langhorn wondered if he had overstepped the line between boss and employee. Then Durham said, ''They're all right as long as they let me do their thinking for them. The way they wrecked that Feeney wagon was handled well enough. By the way, I saw Harding and that sawed-off partner of his deliver the load to Gunderson up at the Rainbow. Gunderson would've told them about not using their line any more." Durham permitted himself a satisfied smile. "We don't have to use any more rough stuff. It'll be easy enough to run them out of business without taking any risks. Nobody will pay them twice as much as I charge, and I happen to know that Feeney's hard pressed for money. If he tries to match my rates, he'll be lucky to last a month."

"After which . . . ?"

"After which my rates go back up again, plus a little extra to cover our losses. Anything else on your mind?"

Langhorn shook his head.

"That's all. I just thought you'd want to know about Dobbs."

"You were right. And now I've got work to do." Without so much as a thank you, he got busy with the papers.

Langhorn left the office, resisting an impulse to slam the door. Sometimes it was hard not to remind Moose that he had known him when he was just a small-time crook.

Harding rode about five miles on the Central City road without finding any spots which looked likely for an ambush. The jolting didn't help the pain in his stomach where Dobbs had hit him, and he decided to go back. Since they would be taking an empty wagon to Central City, it hardly seemed likely that anyone would try to interfere with them. He could look over the rest of the road on the way up. The return trip was what would be hazardous. He must remember to ask Molly where the other wagon had been wrecked.

It was dusk when he approached Leadville. Most of

the stores had already been closed, but light showed from behind the dingy windows of the three saloons, and from the lobby of the hotel. Harding wasn't surprised to find Molly and Frisco still in the office. They looked at him inquiringly, and he shook his head.

"All I found out was that Dobbs hit me pretty hard. We can scout the territory tomorrow on our way to Central City. What time does Mrs. Cook serve supper?"

"Six o'clock," Molly said. "We'll just make it if we leave as soon as you take care of your horse."

"I've been thinking," Frisco Noonan said. "Maybe one of us ought to stay here all night. What do you suppose?"

"Not tonight," Harding said. "Durham probably thinks he's got us licked, with those low rates of his. He'll know better tomorrow when the Courier comes out, but even then I doubt if he'd try burning us out. He's smart enough to realize that that's a two-edged sword." He looked at Molly.

"You know the situation better than we do. What's your opinion?"

"I believe you're right," Molly said. "I don't think breaking the window was Durham's idea. He'd find some trickier way of making trouble."

"Then I'll stable my horse and we can go home. I hope you appreciate having such a noble escort."

"I've been getting back and forth by myself for three years," Molly said. "But since you put it that way . . ."

The wall clock in Hetty Cook's dining room said a minute to six when Molly and the men entered. Stacy Guillford was already at the table, along with a small, intelligent-looking man of about sixty. Guillford made the introductions.

"This is Dr. Mapes. Doc, meet Allan Harding and

Frisco Noonan."

"A pleasure, gentlemen," Dr. Mapes said. "I've been hearing things about you."

Harding flashed a quick look at Guillford, who shook his head.

"Not from me. Folks have to read the *Courier* to find out what I know."

"That's right," Dr. Mapes said. "Mrs. Gagan persuaded her husband to let me look at him. He's the source of my information. He rates you very high."

"That's very kind of him," Harding said. "How's he doing?"

"Well, he'll be pretty sore for a few days, but there's no permanent damage. He wouldn't tell me how it happened."

"Probably he has his reasons," Harding said. "Is your office on the main street? I don't remember noticing your shingle."

"It's in my house, behind the hotel. I don't live here at Mrs. Cook's, in case you're wondering, but ever since my wife died two years ago, I've been eating my suppers here. I'm a terrible cook."

"But a fine doctor," Molly said. "I don't know what Leadville would do without you."

The doctor smiled. "A lot of other places have never heard of me, and they seem to survive, but since I'm the only quack in town, I can claim to be the best. Of course Leadville could exist without me. Folks could always take their aches and pains to Abe Wilkins, at the livery stable. He's a good vet, and when you come right down to it, people aren't so much different from horses."

"Heaven forbid!" Molly exclaimed, and just then Hetty Cook came in with a big bowl of mashed potatoes in one hand, and a platter of roast beef in the other.

"Everybody pitch in. I'll be back with some vegetables. I suppose you all want coffee?"

Nobody voiced an objection, and she went back into the kitchen, to return presently with the vegetables and a pot of coffee.

The meal lived up to expectations, including peach pie. When it was almost over, Hetty's husband, the bartender at the Fast Buck, came into the room, his bald head glistening in the lamplight.

"Heck of a note, ain't it," he said. "I wash glasses all day at the saloon, and then get home just in time to help with the dishes." His grin took the sting from his words. "I see you two fellers liked my recommendation."

"Best advice we've had in months," Harding said. "But I'm afraid Frisco's going to eat up all the profits."

Hetty, who was standing in the kitchen doorway, smiled. "Nothing pleases a cook like seeing a hungry man eat. Joe, if you've talked yourself out, you can give me a hand carrying out the dishes."

Later, in the room they shared, Frisco said as softly as he was able, "I suppose you know I'm still wearing the money belt. Do you intend to ask our landlady to take care of it, or have you changed your mind?"

"I have," Harding said. "Not that I don't trust Mrs. Cook, but it would be putting too much responsibility on her. There must be close to five thousand in it."

"You ain't planning to have me lug it around, are you? I mean now that we've got enemies?"

"Just as far as Central City," Harding said. "There's a bank up there I think we can trust. We'll be making regular trips, or at least I hope so, and can bring it back as we need it." He whirled to face the window. "Did you hear a noise out back?"

Frisco nodded, and they both rushed to the window, but by the time they got it open, the eavesdropper, if there had been one, had disappeared. Harding held the lamp out the window, and they saw a fresh boot print in what was left of the snow. He drew the lamp in, and closed the window, pulling a cloth across it. He and Frisco exchanged looks. It was Harding who spoke.

"I doubt if he heard what we said, but we can't take a chance. One thing certain, you won't be wearing that belt when we go to Central City tomorrow."

"I won't give you an argument on that. But what will we do with it? If the dirty skunk heard us, we can't leave it with Mrs. Cook, even if we wanted to."

"No," Harding agreed. He thought about it a few minutes, and came to a decision.

"If it's all right with you, we'll ask Molly Root's advice. She knows the town, and she's got a good head on her shoulders."

"Suits me," Frisco said and grinned wisely. "You wouldn't by any chance be falling for our silent partner. Would you boy?"

"Of course not," Harding retorted. "It's strictly business."

Somehow, he didn't sound very convincing.

Chapter Ten

Moose Durham's house was situated a block east of Leadville's main street. A two-story structure, made of bricks hauled in from Denver, it was more than big enough to accommodate Durham, his semi-invalid wife Clara, and Lola Marchant, whose position in the household had been well described in Harding's conversation with Mazie Bowen. Lola had been hired personally by Moose, and it was commonly believed that she was his mistress. At any rate she had obviously been chosen more for her physical attributes than for her ability as a housekeeper.

Mrs. Durham was aware of the relationship between Lola and her husband, but pretended not to notice. A naturally timid woman, who had once been pretty, but whose looks had suffered as a result of an undiagnosed illness, she was resigned to the situation, and consoled herself with the thought that she at least had a comfortable home, food to eat, and a husband who would probably continue to provide for her physical needs.

Tonight at supper, Durham had been unusually quiet, paying little attention even to Lola when she served their meal. It was evident that he had something on his mind. Immediately after supper he went to the room which he called his study. About the only studying he did there was figure out ways to make more money.

Foremost on his mind tonight were the new developments at the Feeney Freight Lines. Despite his outward assurance when talking to Ike Langhorn, he was uneasy about Harding and his friend. Harding seemed like a man who would not be easily discouraged. And he did *not* seem like one who would take a job with a business which was headed for disaster. There must be something behind it other than the need for employment. Already, in the short time that he had been here, he had thwarted a plan to interfere with a Feeney wagon, beaten up Dobbs, and had the effrontery to fling down the gauntlet about the broken window.

Durham cursed under his breath. He hated uncertainty. Time was when he would have reacted recklessly by doing something like burn the Feeney barn. Now that he had established himself as a respectable businessman, he had to be more circumspect.

Well, the cut rates ought to do it. There was no law against lowering your prices, even though the obvious purpose was to stifle competition. Feeney wouldn't last long. But where in the devil *was* Feeney? He hadn't been around since shortly after one of his wagons had been wrecked. Why didn't he come back and run the business as he had in the past?

Durham's thoughts were interrupted by a knock on his study door. He yelled, "Come in," and Lola Marchant entered the room.

Durham was in no mood for a woman, even Lola, but before he could send her away, she said, "There's a man asking to see you. Shall I send him in?"

"What's his name, and what does he want?"

"He wouldn't give me his name, but he says he works at the Rainbow mine. He claims it's important."

Mention of the Rainbow was enough to arouse Durham's interest, so he said, "It's probably Gunderson. Let him come in."

Instead of Gunderson, the caller was a young, weak-chinned man who looked as though he was sorry he had come. He gulped nervously, licked his lips, and said uncertainly, "You don't know me, Mr. Durham, but I'm a clerk up at the Rainbow Mine."

"All right, get on with it."

"Yes, sir. You see, Mr. Durham, I overheard something today I thought you might be interested in. I know you cut the rates in half. Well, some fellow from Feeney's was up to the mine with a load, and he agreed to meet your prices. I heard him tell Mr. Gunderson."

"Harding!" Durham snapped. "Was that the man's name?"

"Yes, sir. I heard Mr. Gunderson call him that."

"And whose idea was it for you to bring me the news?"

"Mine. I thought . . ."

"Never mind what you thought. You did the right thing." Durham took out a fat wallet and extracted a ten-dollar bill. "This will pay you for your trouble." He took out another ten. "And this is for keeping your mouth shut about coming here. Understand?"

"Yes, sir," the young man said. "You can depend on it."

"Then be on your way. And be careful not to be seen leaving the house."

After the visitor had left, Durham sat for some time scowling at his desk. He reached for a cigar, stuck it in his mouth, but didn't light it. After a bit he took it out, threw it in the cuspidor, and stood up. If Harding was in a position to make deals like that, he must have authority from Feeney. And Feeney must have raised some money somewhere. Well, there were other ways of handling the situation.

Durham left his study, put on his coat and hat, and hurried out the front door. He went to the freight barn, and knocked on the door to Ike Langhorn's living quarters.

"Open up! It's me, Moose."

Ike's peg leg sounded on the floor, a bolt was thrown, and the door was opened. Langhorn looked up at him. "Something important must have happened to get you down here at night. Have Dobbs and Faraday pulled another dumb stunt?"

"No, dammit, not that I know of. But they're the ones I want to see. That bastard Harding has offered to cut Feeney's rates to match mine."

"I'll be damned. What are you going to do about it?"

"I'm going to teach him a lesson. That's why I want Dobbs and Faraday."

"You think they can handle Harding and his partner?" They haven't done very well so far."

"That isn't my plan. Anyway, all you have to do is get them for me. I imagine they're at the Ace of Spades, but I don't want to be seen talking to them. I'll wait here. Don't come back until you find them."

Langhorn's lips thinned, but he nodded. Putting on his coat and hat, he stomped out into the barn, left through the big doorway, and headed for the main street. Being Durham's errand boy didnt sit well with him, but it was only one more indignity to add to a growing list.

For Harding and Frisco the night passed uneventfully. After breakfast, they and Molly walked together to the Feeney building, which was undamaged. Harding would have built a fire in the office stove, but Molly wouldn't let him.

"I've been doing this myself, and there's no reason to change. I'm not helpless, you know."

"You're an independent hussy," Harding said, grinning. "Since you're so capable, maybe you can do

68

something else. Frisco and I have some cash in a money-belt he's wearing. We'd like a safer place for it. Any ideas?"

She thought about it while she got the fire going, then turned to face him.

"There's no bank in Leadville. Most of the merchants use the stage company's safe, but I wouldn't advise it in your case. My suggestion would be to leave it with Dr. Mapes. He's a privileged character around here, being the only doctor in the area. And I trust him."

"Will you take it to him for us?"

"Of course."

"Thanks. I'll go out in the barn and get it from Frisco. Then we'll hitch up and head for Central City."

"You'll need this paper," Molly said, and handed him one from her desk.

As Harding had predicted, they didn't run into any trouble on the way to Central City. Frisco drove the wagon, and Harding rode his sorrel, scouting the road ahead from time to time, or dropping back to make sure they weren't being followed.

It was dark when they pulled into the livery stable which Molly Root had recommended. The proprietor recognized the wagon, and was surprised at seeing the two men driving it.

"Ain't you the fellers that stabled your horses here a few nights back? Howcome you're driving for Feeney? Is something wrong with Spud Gagan?"

"You're full of questions," Harding said, smiling. "Yes, we spent last Tuesday night here in Central City. We aren't driving for Feeney's. We bought him out. Spud Gagan still works for the company, but he's laid up for a few days. Can you take care of the team and wagon tonight?"

"Reckon so," the man said. "All this is kind of

sudden, ain't it? I mean Feeney selling out and everything?''

"It's sudden, but it's perfectly legal," Harding said. "I can show you the bill of sale if you want to see it."

"Won't be necessary, mister. Just so you pay in advance."

Frisco, cranky from the long ride on a hard wagon seat, when he was more used to a saddle, said to Harding, "Don't you suppose there's another livery barn in town where they know how to treat customers?"

"Now don't get riled," the liveryman said. "I just have to look out for my own interest. After all, you fellers are new in these parts."

Harding, knowing how stubborn Frisco could get, held out a five-dollar bill.

"Let's have less arguing and more action. Rub the horses down good, and see that they're well fed. We'll be making the return trip tomorrow." He turned to Frisco. "Come on, there's still time to get some supper before the restaurant closes. We can stay at the same hotel where we did last time."

After supper, which compared unfavorably with Hetty Cook's meals, the two men took a turn up and down the street. Central City had more night life than Leadville. There were several saloons open, and they chose one at random for a nightcap.

A poker game was in progress, the players three men who wore town clothing, a house dealer rather flashily dressed, and a fresh faced youngster of about twenty. Harding and Feeney, carrying their drinks, moved over to watch the play.

The youngster appeared to have been winning, and was very excited. What made it surprising was that he didn't seem to have much poker sense, at one time drawing to an inside straight. Intrigued, Harding paid closer attention. What he saw didn't please him. In an aside to Frisco he said softly, "That boy's being set up for a killing. I'm going to sit in if they'll let me."

"Why stick your neck out?" Frisco protested. "We all have to learn sometime."

"Let's just say that I hate to see a greenhorn taken advantage of," Harding said. "I bet that boy's never before played for money, and it's a cinch he's never been up against a professional. You might get ready to back me up if there's trouble."

Frisco nodded, and Harding waited for the end of a hand, then asked politely, "Is this a closed game, or can anyone get in?"

They all looked up at him, and one of the older men, whose stack of chips was very low, said with relief, "You can have my seat. This just isn't my night."

"Thanks," Harding said, and took the vacated chair. He slid a twenty-dollar bill across to the dealer, and received his chips. The dealer looked at him closely, but didn't introduce himself. He said mechanically, "It's five-card stud, and table limits."

"Fair enough," Harding said, and anted. His hole card proved to be a seven of hearts.

The youngster was at Harding's left. Apparently his first card was a good one, and he did a poor job of concealing his elation. Probably an ace, Harding surmised.

Harding's second card, face up, was another seven, an the youngster got a deuce of clubs. His elation faded.

One of the other men was dealt a king, which topped the board. He shoved out a dollar chip, and everybody covered it, Harding realizing that if he raised, they would guess that he had a pair.

By the fourth card, only Harding, the youngster, and the dealer remained in the game. Harding hadn't improved his pair, and the youngster had nothing showing higher than an eight spot. The dealer was high with a pair of nines showing. He shoved five chips into the pot, Harding called, and the greenhorn, with nothing worthwhile except a possible high-hole card, very unwisely called. His chance of matching his hole card and beating the dealer's pair was remote.

The last deal brought Harding another seven, the youngster a five of hearts, and the dealer a jack of diamonds. He pushed out another five chips, Harding called, and the young man, finally showing some sense, folded. Harding took the pot. So far he had not seen anything wrong, though it did seem odd that his entrance into the game had broken the boy's streak of good luck.

The next few hands were not especially lucky for anyone, and there was little change in the stacks of chips. Then the boy began to get lucky again. He won two pots in a row, and on the next deal had a pair of queens showing, with one card yet to come. Harding had folded, and the dealer showed a pair of deuces. The youngster, hardly able to control himself, shoved all his chips into the middle of the table. Anyone could guess that he had a third queen in the hole.

"Have to keep you honest," the dealer said, and matched the bet. He dealt the boy a six of clubs. He was about to deal to himself, when Harding's hand shot out and grabbed his wrist.

"Just a minute, if you don't mind. I'd like to make a side bet. All my chips that there's a deuce in the hole, and another on the bottom of the deck."

The dealer's face flushed, and he said viciously, "Are you calling me a cheat?"

Harding shrugged. "Just offering a side bet. What's wrong with that?"

"Why damn you!" The dealer shook a derringer out of his sleeve. Before he could aim it, he was looking down the barrel of Harding's sixgun.

"Don't try it," Harding warned. "Just lay your pea-shooter on the table real easy. That's right. Now we'll have a look at that bottom card." He reached out his left hand, turned over the pack, and exposed a deuce. "Does anyone want to bet that he doesn't have the fourth deuce for his hole card?"

Nobody spoke. In fact the whole room had gone silent. Harding said thinly, "There's nothing much lower than a crooked dealer. The pot's yours, son. Cash in your chips, and after this be more suspicious of good luck."

Red-faced, the boy watched the dealer buy back his chips. He put the money in his pocket, stood up, and unexpectedly grabbed the dealer by the shirt front, pulled him up out of his chair, and slammed a fist into his jaw. The dealer crumpled like a wet sack.

Over to one side, Frisco said gleefully, "Son of a gun! He can't play poker for cold beans, but he sure packs a punch."

Harding stood up and looked around at the bartender. "Any objections to what I did, mister?"

The bartender didn't answer, and Harding said to nobody in particular and everybody in general, "I suggest that you run this crooked dealer out of town." He motioned to the youngster, and added, "Come on, boy, you'd better stick with my partner and me for a while."

"Yes, sir," the boy said. When the three of them were outside the saloon, he added embarrassedly, "I guess I was making an awful fool of myself. Thanks for what you did."

"That's all right," Harding said. "What's your

name?"

"Billy Gregg."

"Well, Billy, this is Frisco Noonan, and I'm Allan Harding. What're you doing in Central City?"

"I'm on my way to Leadville," Billy said, "Back in Nebraska, I heard they were hiring men in the mines."

"I'm afraid you heard wrong," Harding said. "But if you're not determined to be a miner, maybe you'd consider something else."

"Anything except playing poker," Billy said, and Harding laughed.

"Can you handle a team and wagon?"

"That's one thing I *can* do," Billy said. "I grew up on a farm."

"Then how would you like to work for us? We have a freighting outfit. I'd better warn you, though, before you say yes, that there may be some danger involved."

"That doesn't bother me. Not much, anyway."

"Good. You can ride back with us tomorrow. Where are you staying?"

"At the Rex Hotel."

"Then you'd better move over to the Colorado. I think we ought to stick together." He looked at Frisco.

"Does this sound all right to you, partner?"

"Sure," Frisco said. "Anybody who can punch like Billy is tops in my book. Now let's get going. I'm sleepy."

Chapter Eleven

The following day dawned raw and cloudy, with the threat of more snow. Harding and his two companions were up early, went to a cafe for breakfast, and reached the livery barn by six-thirty. While Frisco and Billy hitched up the team, Harding settled his account with the liveryman, who was more agreeable than the night before. He even volunteered a little information.

"A couple other freighters pulled out of here two hours ago. They'd loaded their wagon last night."

"Did you notice the name on the wagon."

"Sure. Anyway, I've seen it lots of times before. It was Rocky Mountain Freight Co."

"What did the men look like?"

"One of them was tall and stringy; the other was about my size. Why? Do you know them?"

"I might," Harding said, and turned away. He saddled his sorrel, and by then the wagon was ready to roll. Frisco, beside Billy on the wagon seat, looked at Harding curiously.

"Why the frown? Did the liveryman give you a bad time?"

"No, but he gave me some information I don't like. Dobbs and Faraday pulled out with a load a couple of hours ago. I didn't think they were drivers. They seemed more like hardcases. Well, let's get over to the warehouse and load up." He looked at Billy.

"Do you have any kind of gun, boy?"

"No, sir," Billy said. "I never owned a pistol, and I left my rifle in Nebraska. Why? Should I have one?"

"Have you done much shooting?"

"Yes, sir. I can pick off a squirrel at a hundred yards."

"Well, you won't be seeing many squirrels on this trip, but we might bump into a couple of skunks. After we load up, we'll locate a gun shop and try to pick up a secondhand rifle."

The warehouse wasn't hard to find, since Molly had given them specific directions. It was already open for business, and a mild-looking man wearing a canvas apron asked politely, "What'll it be, stranger?"

Harding took out the paper Molly had given him, and handed it over. The man looked at it and frowned.

"There must be some mistake. This stuff was picked up last night."

"Picked up! By who?"

A couple of fellers with a Rocky Mountain wagon."

"One tall and the other short?"

"That's right, but I can do better than that. I know their names. They were Dobbs and Faraday."

"How come you gave the shipment to them? Did they have a pickup order?"

"Yes, sir. They said your company has been taken over by Rocky Mountain. Hasn't it?"

"No," Harding said. "And if they pull this stunt again, don't let them fool you. By rights you could be held liable for giving our goods to somebody else."

"Confound it, I had no way of knowing. Rocky Mountain has picked up supplies here lots of times. I had no reason to think they were up to something crooked. I'm sorry."

"Yes," Harding said. "We all are. I suppose it was an honest mistake on your part, so forget what I said about your being liable. Just don't let it happen again."

He turned away to face Frisco and Billy, who had been

listening to the conversation.

"They've got a good start on us, but we'll make better time with an empty wagon. That Durham is a tricky devil. You two head for Leadville. I'll buy Billy a rifle and catch up with you."

Frisco nodded, and put the team in motion. The wagon had gone perhaps three miles when Harding overtook it. He handed Billy a rifle and box of cartridges.

"Remember I warned you that this job might be dangerous. Frisco can tell you what's happened so far. I'm going to ride out front and see if I can catch sight of them."

"Yes, sir," Billy said, and began loading the rifle. He didn't look scared, just excited.

Harding had ridden five miles when it started to snow, at first just a few lazy flakes, but soon a thick blanket. It was a mixed blessing. He couldn't see far ahead, but on the other hand, if he got close to Dobbs and Faraday he would be able to see their wagon tracks. Of course he had to keep a sharp lookout. One of the men could have gotten off the wagon and be waiting to ambush him. After considering this several minutes, he pulled off the road and took a parallel route to one side, being careful to stay close enough to spot either the wagon or an ambusher.

Presently the terrain forced him back onto the road, which at this point was carved out of the side of a hill, with a steep upslope on one side, and a deep arroyo on the other. For the first time he saw wagon tracks in the snow. They had filled in enough so that he knew he wasn't close. The two hardcases were making good time for a loaded wagon.

Back at the Feeney wagon, Frisco and Billy had turned up their coat collars and were thoroughly uncomfortable. Frisco, having told Billy some of the things which had happened since their arrival in Leadville, had subsided into a glum silence, mentally cursing the climate, Moose Durham, and the world in general. Why couldn't he and Allan have gone down into Arizona, where there would be warmth and sunshine? For two cents . . . No, he wouldn't pull out. He and Harding had been friends too long for that. Harding had saved his life more than once, and he could remember a couple of occasions on which he had returned the favor.

Billy, although he must be as miserable as Frisco, was bright eyed and alert. It was he who first spotted the tracks of the other wagon and called them to Frisco's attention.

"They're pretty faint," Billy said. "The wagon must be quite a ways ahead of us. I wonder where Mr. Harding is."

"Lord knows," Frisco said. "I hope he doesn't take them on alone."

About noon, Harding spotted the Rocky Mountain wagon through a rift in the snow. It had stopped, presumably to give the horses a breather, and he was lucky not to have ridden right up to it. The land had leveled off again, after passing the arroyo, and there were scrubby pines beside the road. Harding pulled in behind one of them, hoping he hadn't been seen.

They must be expecting to be followed, so they would surely be looking back from time to time. This made it impossible to approach close enough to get the drop on them. And he was sure they would have rifles or carbines, which took away his advantage.

Although the snow had closed in again, blocking vision, Harding was near enough to hear their voices. Presently there was the pop of a whip, followed by the creaking of wheels. Harding waited for the sound to fade, then turned back toward Central City. After half an hour he came close to the wagon driven by Frisco. Billy had his rifle at his shoulder, and Harding called a warning.

"It's me, Harding. Hold your fire!"

Billy lowered the gun, and Harding waited for the wagon to come up to him. Frisco drew the team to a stop and said gruffly, "What's up? Have you seen the two polecats?"

"They're about five miles ahead of us," Harding said, and this made Frisco straighten up from his hunched position.

"Let's get on with it then. There's three of us against two. We can take 'em. Right, Billy?"

"Yes, sir," Billy said, then added, "I guess so."

"Not so fast," Harding cautioned. "Like you say, we've got them outgunned, but that won't stop them from shooting. One of us is liable to get hurt, or if not us, one of the horses. I have another idea. You follow along like you have been until you see them. It's all right if they see you, too, but keep out of range."

"And what'll you be doing?" Frisco demanded.

"I'm going to try to get ahead of them. If you hear two shots, close together, come in fast. Okay?"

"Whatever you say," Frisco said. "Just so we get it over with. I want to get someplace where I can thaw out."

"Just keep your mind on Dobbs and Faraday," Harding said, "and how they slickered us out of our load. That ought to warm you up. Billy, are you all right?"

"Yes, sir," Billy said. "I'm fine."

"Good. Only you don't have to keep calling me 'sir.' Frisco, don't try to catch up with the wagon until you

79

hear those two shots. It may be some time." Without waiting for an answer, he turned his horse, and headed off in the direction of Leadville. When he reached the point at which the wagon had stood, he pulled off the road and took to higher ground. After an hour he was rewarded with the creaking of wagon wheels and muffled sound of hoofs. He rode on past, careful to keep out of sight, which wasn't difficult on account of the falling snow. Not for another hour did he angle back to the road.

There was very little cover here, but Harding found a clump of cedar beside the road. He dismounted, tied his sorrel to a branch, and slid the carbine out of his saddle scabbard.

Presently he heard the sound of the approaching wagon. He waited as long as he dared, then stepped out into the road, fired a warning shot in the air, and called sharply, "Hold it right there! You're already in my sights."

Dobbs let out a surprised curse, but he pulled the team to a stop. "Harding?"

"That's right. You thought I'd be behind you, didn't you? A natural mistake, at least for a man with no brains. Get off the wagon, both of you."

At this short distance, Harding could see the expressions on their faces. Dobbs looked furious, but Faraday appeared unconcerned. He would be the one to watch. Both men clambered down from the wagon seat and stood beside the left front wheel.

"Now shed your guns," Harding said. "Just drop them in the road. Faraday, get the rifles out of the wagon."

They hesitated, and Harding fired two quick shots over their heads. This served the dual purpose of making them comply, and signaling Frisco and Billy.

80

Harding moved up closer.

"It seems there was a little mixup in Central City. You were given our load by mistake. Funny, isn't it?"

Apparently neither of them could see any humor in the situation, for they didn't smile. Harding heard the other wagon approaching, and waited for it to pull alongside. Without turning his head, he said, "These two gentlemen just discovered that they have our load of freight. They're about to volunteer to shift it to our wagon."

"You son of a bitch!" Dobbs snarled.

"I like you, too," Harding said pleasantly. "Now get moving. The faster you work, the sooner you'll be done. Billy, gather up their artillery and toss it in our wagon, under the seat. Frisco, hold a gun on these men."

"With pleasure," Frisco said, and drew his revolver.

Cursing and fuming, Dobbs and Faraday transferred the load to the Feeney wagon. When they had finished, and the canvas was tied down, Harding said, "Now unhitch your team."

"Wait a damn minute! You ain't going to leave us stranded out here on foot!"

"Just do as you're told," Harding said, and the two men unwillingly complied. Harding reached out for the cheek strap of the nearest horse.

"By rights we ought to wreck the wagon, like you did one of Feeney's last month, but we're naturally kindly individuals. Besides, we appreciate your generous offer to shift the load. You'll find your horses a few miles down the road. The walk will do you good."

"Moose Durham ain't going to sit still for this," Faraday warned.

"No, I imagine he won't," Harding said. "He likely doesn't care for his men to make mistakes. But you'll probably dream of some kind of explanation. Good luck." He motioned to Billy.

"Billy, you can ride one of the horses and lead the other. It'll be a nice change from a hard wagon seat."

"You bet!" Billy said. He got up on one of the horses and seized the bridle of the other.

Harding went to his sorrel, and stepped into the saddle. He motioned for Frisco to drive ahead, and turned for one last look at the two disgusted hardcases.

"Thanks for hauling our load over half the distance to Leadville. We'll do the same for you someday. And give my regards to your boss."

"Go to hell!" Dobbs said, but Faraday merely laughed. When Harding looked back a few minutes later, they had started to walk.

Chapter Twelve

Once again it was dusk when Harding and the other two reached Leadville, but this time most of the stores were open. Harding remembered it was Saturday, the traditional day to blow off steam after a week of hard work. He had observed it many times in various cattle towns, when the cowboys rode in to celebrate and get a little drunk. Probably miners shared the same instincts. Mazie's place would be busy, too.

Regretfully, Harding realized that they would be too late for supper at Hetty Cook's. He was surprised to find a light still burning at the Feeney barn, and Molly watching out the window. She greeted him in the office doorway.

"Did everything go all right?"

"Not exactly," Harding said, stepping out of the saddle. "But it turned out fair enough. Frisco is right behind me with the wagon. By the way, we hired another driver in Central City."

"Whatever for?" Molly asked. "After what came out yesterday in the *Courier*, Moose Durham is going to be even more determined to run you out of business. He'll use every dirty trick in the book."

"He's already used one," Harding said, "and it backfired." He told her about the misdirected load. "Luckily, we caught up with Dobbs and Faraday, and they kindly consented to rectify the error."

"At the point of a gun?"

"Well, yes," Harding admitted. "But nobody got shot. I suppose we missed supper?"

"Good heavens! After what happened today, you can still worry about food? All right, Hetty agreed to save you something in the warming oven. But about this man you hired, what's he like?"

"Young. About your age, I'd guess, and fresh off a Nebraska farm. You can't help liking him. His name is Billy Gregg. Here comes the wagon now, so you can see him for yourself."

Frisco lifted a hand in greeting as the wagon came into the barn, and Billy's eyes popped at sight of Molly Root. They drove through to the back of the barn. Harding grinned at Molly.

"Methinks you've already made a conquest. Don't let him down too hard; he's a nice boy."

"I can see that," Molly said. "Where will he stay? Mrs. Cook doesn't have any vacant rooms."

"I've been thinking about that, among other things. Maybe he can bunk right here in this building, and take his meals at Hetty's. It wouldn't be such a bad idea to have someone here nights anyway."

"But won't it be dangerous for him? I mean if Moose Durham, or one of his roughnecks tries to cause trouble?"

"We've already decided that Durham won't attack the building for fear we'll do the same thing to his. Besides, Billy's no fool. Young, maybe, but he won't be a pushover. And he has a gun, in case he needs it. Tell me, did you get rid of the moneybelt?"

"Yes. Dr. Mapes is keeping it for you."

Frisco and Billy came into the office just then. Frisco hurried over to the stove, but Billy stood diffidently just inside the doorway. Harding motioned him over, and said to Molly, "This is Billy Gregg, the new man I was telling you about. Billy, meet Molly Root, the brains of the outfit."

"Pleased to meet you, miss," Billy said. Apparently he saw something in Molly's eyes which gave him encouragement, for he added, "Frisco's been telling me about you, but he didn't say . . ."

"Didn't say *what*?" Molly asked.

"Nothing," Billy mumbled. "Excuse me, I think I'll go over and get warmed up."

What Billy had been about to say was that Frisco hadn't told him Molly was so young and pretty. Any misgivings he had had about taking the job vanished. He saw Frisco grinning at him, and his face reddened.

"Well," Molly said. "If you men want some supper, we'd better get moving. Hetty won't keep it much longer."

They found Stacy Guillford in the kitchen with Mrs. Cook, drinking coffee. Harding made the introductions, and Mrs. Cook looked at Billy with a motherly expression.

"You must be starved. Sit down there at the table and I'll load you a plate."

"Yes'm," Billy said respectfully.

Frisco said in mock injured tones, "Does that go for me too, even if I ain't young and good-looking?"

"It was meant to include all of you," Hetty said, smiling. "Even you, grumpy."

"So I'm grumpy, am I?" Frisco said, looking not at all offended. "By gum you would be, too, if you'd been riding through a snow storm all day on a hard plank."

Hetty laughed and began serving the plates. It occurred to Harding that she didn't know the meaning of small helpings. The food was bountiful as well as good.

Molly didn't linger, but went to her room. However Guillford waited until there was an opportunity, then said to Harding, "I'd like a word with you when you finish. Maybe we could take a walk through the business block. You haven't seen Leadville on a Saturday night."

"A good idea," Harding said, although he would gladly have gone to bed. He finished his meal and stood up. "Let's go now. I aim to turn in pretty early."

As they left the house, and were out of the hearing of the others, Guillford said soberly, "I had a visit from Moose Durham yesterday after the paper came out. He didn't like that ad of yours."

"That's understandable," Harding said. "But he surely didn't blame you for printing it, did he?"

"Not in so many words," Guillford said. "However, he dopped a hint that he was thinking of cutting down on his advertising. That could mean quite a loss in revenue, since he controls several businesses in town besides the freighting company."

"Good Lord!" Harding exclaimed. "I didn't mean to get you in hot water. I always thought that anyone was entitled to advertise whatever he pleased."

"I still think so," Guillford said. "But Durham isn't used to being crossed. I just thought I'd let you know."

"I won't put any ad in the paper this coming week," Harding said. "There's no point dragging you into our private war."

"But I'm already in," Guillford said. "You see, I told Durham I intended to run the newspaper my way, without outside interference. You can imagine how that set with him. But I'm not going to be dictated to by anyone, not even him. I happen to believe in a free press. I told Durham so."

"Did he make any threats?"

"Not directly. Except the threat of discontinuing his advertising."

"How much does that amount to?" Harding asked.

"In square inches or however you figure it."

"About one full page, give or take a little. Or around fifty dollars a week."

They had reached the business section, and passed the unlighted window of Moose Durham's office. There was considerable activity along the rest of the street, buggies and wagons next to the sidewalk, saddlehorses at the saloons hitchrails. Folks from the surrounding area had come to town to do their weekly shopping, miners and settlers to visit the bars. Harding and Guillford were passing a narrow alley between two buildings when there was the sound of a gun being cocked. Without hesitation, Harding flung himself against his companion, knocking him off his feet. As he did, a gun roared, and Guillford gasped.

Harding rose to his feet and looked down at Guillford. "Are you hurt bad?"

"I don't think so," Guillford said. "But my left arm feels numb." He tried to sit up, and Harding helped him.

"If you're able to walk, we'd better get you over to Doc Mapes. Can you make it?"

"I can try," Guillford said, and rose shakily to his feet. He appeared weak.

By now quite a crowd had gathered, standing around as crowds do without offering to help. Harding pointed to a buggy near by.

"Does that rig belong to any of you folks?"

"It's mine," a man said.

"Well, I'm borrowing it to take this man to the doctor. You can come along if you want to, or pick it up over there."

"Now just a minute," the man protested, but Harding ignored him. He got Guillford into the buggy, picked up the weight and set it on the floor, and moved in beside him. Unwrapping the lines from the whipstock, he put the horse into motion. Minutes later he was half carrying Guillford up Dr. Mapes's path.

"Open the door, Doc. It's me, Harding."

The door was jerked open, and Harding led Guillford inside. Dr. Mapes didn't waste time asking questions, but started taking off Guillford's coat. He eased the man down onto a table and bent over him. Presently he straightened up.

"It doesn't appear to be serious. Just a flesh wound. You'll have a stiff arm for a few days, Mr. Guillford. Not good for a man setting type."

"It's a lot better than it would have been if Mr. Harding hadn't acted fast," Guillford said. "Confound a man who'll shoot from ambush!"

Harding remained silent while Dr. Mapes cleaned the wound and bandaged it. By then Guillford had recovered enough to smile. "I'm obliged to you, Harding. I didn't even know anything was wrong until you pushed me."

"Maybe you don't owe me any thanks," Harding said. "It could be that I pushed you into the line of fire."

'What do you mean?"

"The bushwhacker could have been shooting at me," Harding explained. "I've made more enemies around here than you have. It's odd, though . . ."

"What's odd?" Guillford asked.

"Well, I'd naturally suspect Dobbs and Faraday, but I don't see how they could possibly be in town yet. We left them stranded on the Central City road five miles from their horses."

Guillford frowned. "Maybe I'm delirious, but I don't understand what you're talking about. What do you mean, stranded?"

"It's a long story," Harding told him, smiling. "Maybe I'll let you in on it later." He broke off abruptly, and was silent for a few seconds before adding, "Tell me something, Guillford. Did you really mean that about a free press?"

"Absolutely."

"Then I've got a front-page story for next week's *Courier*. It'll make Durham mad as hell, but it'll sell copies. And about the advertising—I'll give you a full-page ad that will cover the fifty dollars for at least one week."

"Oh come on, you don't have to do that."

"But I do. If someone's shooting at us, whether it was you or me he was after, the war's on. I don't intend to be scared out. Of course what you do is your decision to make. I can't make you print the story or publish my ad."

"Just try to stop me, and see how far you get," Guillford said. "I don't like being shot at any better than you do. Or being threatened by a man like Moose Durham. Besides, what have I got to lose? I've no family, and only a hole-in-the-wall print shop." He held out his hand. "Agreed?"

"Agreed," Harding said. "You're a good man to have on my side." He turned to Dr. Mapes. "Is Guillford all right to go now?"

"Certainly," Dr. Mapes said. "But from the way you've been talking, I'll be expecting you back before long. Mr. Guillford, I'm going to give you some pills, in case the pain keeps you awake. Come back tomorrow and let me look at your arm."

"Sure, Doc," Guillford said, and got down from the table.

When they went outside, the buggy was gone. In view of Guillford's condition, they decided to dispense with the rest of the tour. There would be other Saturday nights, Harding told himself.

Or would there? A gunman, identity unknown, was on the loose. Maybe next time he wouldn't miss.

Chapter Thirteen

Since it was Saturday, Moose Durham, unaware of
what had happened on the road, had left his office and
gone home for an early supper. He intended to go back
to the barn afterward, and make sure that Dobbs and
Faraday had come through all right with the purloined
load of merchandise. Not that he anticipated trouble.
Dobbs and Faraday were experienced at this sort of
thing, and should be more than a match for Harding
and his battered old partner.

After supper he went into his study for a fresh supply
of cigars. Before long Lola Marchant entered the room
without knocking. She had changed from her house
dress to a seductively low-necked garment. She smiled at
him conspiratorially.

"I put one of those powders in her tea. She'll sleep
through the night."

Durham, torn between two desires, said thickly,
"You ought to check with me before doing that. I'm
going to be leaving in a few minutes."

"You'll be back, won't you? We have plenty of
time."

'Oh sure, I'll be back." Moved by a passion he
couldn't control, he drew her close and kissed her
hungrily. With an effort of will he thrust her away from
him and said hoarsely, "I'll make it as soon as I can.
But about those powders, you'd better be careful how
you use them. The effect might wear off."

"Oh, I've been giving her a little more each time," Lola said.

"That could be dangerous. She might not wake up."

"So?" Lola said, shrugging. "Everybody knows she's a sick woman. If she were to die, they'd be around offering sympathy. And nobody would say anything if you kept the same housekeeper. After a while we could get married."

"I've never promised you that," Durham said. "You're taking too much for granted."

"We'll see," Lola said, and left the room.

Durham had never seriously considered doing away with his wife, but now that Lola had put the idea in his mind, he couldn't brush it away. Suddenly he felt the need for fresh air. With a curse he put on his coat and hat and hurried out of the house. He reached the main street just in time to see the Feeney wagon enter its barn. There were two men in the seat. In the dim light, he assumed that they were Harding and his friend.

Something had obviously gone wrong. Tight-lipped, Durham went to his own barn, where he found Ike Langhorn checking over the horses. Langhorn looked around at him and said, "Dobbs and Faraday are overdue. Something must have gone haywire."

"I know," Durham said. "I just saw the Feeney wagon pull in with a full load. By God that Harding's too smart for his own good! First he puts an ad in the *Courier*, then he gets the best of two of my men. He's building himself up for an accident."

Langhorn looked at him thoughtfully. "Does that mean what I think it does, Moose?"

"Do I have to spell it out?"

Langhorn didn't answer, but Durham's meaning was plain enough. The strawboss moved out of the stall he had been checking. Matter of factly he said, "There's nobody but me to watch the barn. Do you feel like hanging around till I get back?"

"I'll stay," Durham said. "But what are you planning to do? Harding will probably go to Mrs. Cook's and turn in. You can't do anything tonight."

"Don't be too sure," Langhorn said. "Harding and the other one have a room on the back of the house, with a window close to the ground. I know, because Faraday was up there a couple of nights ago trying to hear what they were talking about. Speaking of Faraday, we're liable not to see him or Dobbs any more. If they're this late, they may be dead."

Durham didn't comment, and Langhorn left the barn. An hour later, Durham heard a single gunshot, and a satisfied smile twisted his lips. There would be no more trouble with Harding. He took out a cigar, and had just got it going when Langhorn stumped into the office, looking frustrated.

"I missed. The lucky bastard is still alive."

Langhorn's expression was such that Durham wisely held back what was on the tip of his tongue. Instead, he said bluntly, "Tell me what went wrong."

"Well, I watched the boardng house, thinking I might get Harding in his room. Instead, he and Guillford came out the front door together and headed downtown. They were moving slow, so it was easy for me to follow them. when I saw that they were going to walk along this side of the street, I got ahead of them, going behind the store buildings, and went into that alleyway next to the feed store. I could hear their voices, but when they showed up, I must've made some sound. Harding knocked Guillford down, but not before I got off a shot. It hit one of them, but it was Guillford, not Harding."

"Kill him?" Durham asked, and Langhorn shook his

head.

"Guillford was able to get to his feet afterward. I circled around the store and saw Harding help him into a buggy. By that time there was so much of a crowd that all I could do was come back to the barn."

"Well, let's hope you put Guillford out of action for a while. That'll leave nobody to publish the paper. I wonder where the hell Dobbs and Faraday are. If they're alive, that is."

The two men he was wondering about were alive, and had almost reached Leadville. It had taken them over two hours to recover their wagon horses, ride back and hitch them up, and get under way. Both of them were cold and angry, although Faraday was able to see the humor of the situation. Overriding their anger was worry as to how they would explain things to Durham.

The latter was still in the barn when they drove in. He scowled at them accusingly.

"Let's have it, and no lying. How did you manage to mess things up this time?"

Dobbs had mentally prepared an explanation which wouldn't make them look so bad, but Durham's tone of voice scared it out of him, and he said, "There was three of them, not just two, only we didn't know it at first. They was close enough behind us so that we could see two men on their wagon. We figured it to be Harding and that old man he runs around with. When Harding popped up in front of us, we didn't have a chance.."

"Go on. What happened next?"

"Well, they took away our guns, and made us shift the load to their wagon. It was hard work, believe me, what with the snow and everything. Then they unhitched our team and led the horses five miles down the road and left them. Getting them back was what took us so long."

94

It sounded like a straightforward explanation, and Durham decided to accept it. "This third man, what can you tell me about him?"

"Just that he wasn't much more than a kid," Faraday said. "I heard one of them call him Billy."

"Well, put up the rig and take care of the horses. There's nothing more you can do tonight. In the morning get yourselves some more guns. I'll have Ike let you know when I want you."

Relieved at having been let off so easily, Dobbs and Faraday drove farther back into the barn, and unharnessed the team. An hour later they were at the Ace of Spades. Most of the folks from outlying areas had left for home, but there were several regulars there. Marshal Banks was present, belatedly asking questions about the shooting of Guillford. He claimed to have been at the other end of town when it had happened. Everyone believed him, for that was where Mazie Brown's place was. He noticed the two Durham men and moved over to face them.

"Where were you when it happened?"

"When what happened?" Faraday asked quickly, forestalling an incautious answer by Dobbs. "We drove into town just half an hour ago. Did we miss some excitement?"

"Did anyone see you drive in?"

"Hell, yes. There must've been a dozen people on the street."

"I saw them," the hotelman volunteered. "They didn't show up until an hour after the shooting."

"Shooting? Who got shot?" Dobbs asked, honestly mystified.

"Stacy Guillford," Marshal Banks said. "I'm trying to find out who did it. When I do, it'll go hard on him."

Having spoken his piece, Banks left the saloon. He

had made an effort. Nobody could accuse him of neglecting his duty. Of course he had no expectation of identifying the ambusher. Almost anyone could have sneaked into that passageway and fired the shot, especially on a night like this, when the town was full of people. In the morning he would ask a few more questions, but he didn't expect to learn anything. In fact he didn't want to. The logical person to have a grudge against Harding and Guillford was Moose Durham: Harding because he was challenging Durham's freighting business, and Guillford for publishing that ad.

The marshal's dream of going back to Mazie's place had to be abandoned when he ran into Harding outside the saloon. Harding moved in front of him to block his path.

"Glad I found you, Marshal. I was on my way to your office. Have you uncovered anything about the shooting?"

"Not much," Banks said. "Except that it wasn't Dobbs or Faraday. After that ruckus you had in the Mexicali, I thought it might be Dobbs."

"Dobbs isn't a suspect," Harding said. "Or the other one, either."

"No? How come you know so much about it?"

"They were both out of town when it happened," Harding said. "Unless they've sprouted wings, that is, which I doubt. Did you look for tracks between the two buildings?"

"Of course. I don't need you to tell me how to do my job." He started to walk around Harding, but Harding moved in front of him again.

"You see, Marshal, I'm personally involved in this. It always bothers me when someone tries to kill me. Let's go back and have another look for those tracks. Surely you aren't in that much of a hurry."

The marshal thought fleetingly of Mazie Bowen's house, then forced it out of his mind. If he refused to go back, Harding would make it look as though he were shirking his duty. He muttered an oath and said grudgingly, "All right. I'll borrow a lantern from the saloon. Be right back."

Harding moved over to the grimy window, saw Banks say something to the bartender, after which the bartender reached up for one of the lighted lanterns over the bar. Harding also noticed Dobbs and Faraday, but he had nothing new to discuss with them. Then the marshal came back onto the street, holding a lantern by its loop.

"Damned waste of time, if you ask me, but come on."

They entered the passageway from which the shot had been fired, the marshal holding the lantern shoulder high. When they reached the approximate point from which the shot had seemed to come, Harding took hold of Banks's arm.

"Don't go so fast. We don't want to blot out any prints."

"What the hell. I've already made tracks all over here."

Harding took the lantern from him and held it close to the ground. After a few minutes he straightened up.

"Are you sure this is where you looked?"

"Of course I'm sure. Plenty of folks told me where the shots came from."

"That's strange," Harding said. "I can't see any tracks at all, not even yours. It looks as though the place has been swept clean."

"Let me see," Banks said, and took back the lantern. After a bit he turned to face Harding, his brow furrowed.

"I don't get it. Why would anybody pull a stunt like that?"

"I wish I knew," Harding said, as puzzled as the marshal. "Before you were here, yes, but afterward. . . ? Well, there's nothing more to be found out here until daylight. Thanks for your cooperation."

"You're not welcome," Banks said. "And from now on, you tend to your job and let me tend to mine. Amateurs just get in the way."

"So I've noticed," Harding said, and led the way out of the alleyway.

Frisco was lying on the bed, fully dressed, when Harding entered the bedroom. He looked up at Harding curiously.

"Where the blazes did you run off to? I've been worried."

"You needn't have been," Harding said. "I just went out to look for footprints between those two store buildings. The marshal, after a little coaxing, agreed to accompany me."

"And what did you find?"

"Nothing. Not a single footprint. Not even the marshal's, and he claimed to have been there earlier. Someone took a broom to the place."

"So what did you do about it?"

"Not much I could do," Harding said. "I came on home. Oh, I did make one stop on the way. I got to thinking about those guns we took away from Dobbs and Faraday. They really don't belong in our barn. We might even be accused of stealing them."

"So?"

"So I got them out of our wagon and returned them to Moose Durham."

Frisco jerked erect.

"You took them to his house?"

"No," Harding said solemnly. "I took them to his office. Unfortunately, the office was closed and locked. I did the only decent thing."

"Don't tell me," Frisco said, grinning. "You shoved them through the window, which was also closed."

"That's right," Harding acknowledged, matching Frisco's grin with one of his own. "Which makes us even. They broke our window, and now we've broken theirs. Anyway, Durham ought to thank me for returning the guns so promptly."

"Oh, he'll thank you all right," Frisco said drily. "Probably with a forty-five slug in the guts. Are you coming to bed, or ain't you?"

"Be right there," Harding said. "I'm sleepy."

"So was I, half an hour ago," Frisco said. "But now I ain't so sure."

Chapter Fourteen

When Harding woke up, Frisco was shaving, a regular Sunday ritual. Harding held his silence as long as he could, then asked, "Why don't you use soap to soften your whiskers?"

"Makes 'em grow faster," Frisco said. "Don't be telling me how to shave. I was doing it before you was born."

"Someday . . ."

"Someday *what*?"

"Well, I was just thinking. Someday the right woman will come along, and she'll have you shaving every day and twice on Sundays."

"Hogwash!" Frisco scoffed. "Now you've made me cut myself!"

They went down to breakfast together, and found all the other boarders at the table, including Stacy Guillford with his left arm in a sling. Harding took a double look at Molly Root, who was wearing a flowered dress instead of her usual Levi's and jacket, and who had let down her hair around her shoulders. She looked prettier and younger, in fact much younger. It made Harding feel old.

Dr. Mapes was at his usual place, Sunday being the only day on which he came to Mrs. Cook's for breakfast; and Billy Gregg, having come from the freight barn, was sitting next to him, directly across the table from Molly. They all exchanged good mornings, and Hardy asked Molly, "How come the fancy duds?"

"Because it's Sunday," Molly said. "I'm going to church."

"Church? In Leadville? I haven't noticed anything that looked like a church building."

"We hold services in the school house," Molly said. "You'll be welcome if you care to attend. You and Frisco both."

Frisco choked on a swallow of coffee, and Harding said, "Thanks just the same, but we have other things to tend to. Shouldn't those supplies be delivered?"

"The receiving clerk won't be there today," Molly said. "Or anybody to pay you the freighting charges. It'll have to wait till tomorrow."

Billy Gregg, wearing a clean shirt and with his hair slicked down, cleared his throat nervously. "I'd just as lief go to church, if it's all right."

"Why of course," Molly said, smiling. "We can go together if you like. It won't be for another two hours, though."

Hetty Cook came in from the kitchen just then, bringing plates of food for the latest arrivals. She looked at Frisco in mock surprise, and asked Harding, "Who's the stranger? I don't remember seeing him before."

"You haven't," Harding said. "He's been hiding behind a bush. He's like a groundhog, only he comes out once a week instead of once a year."

"Have yourselves a good time," Frisco said. "So long as you give me plenty of flapjacks and bacon." He glanced at Guillford.

"How's the arm?"

"Not bad, so far as I can tell," Guillford said. "Doc Mapes is going to look at it after breakfast. Right, Doc?"

"That's correct," Dr. Mapes said. "And then I have

101

to pay a call on Mrs. Durham. She likes me to drop by on Sunday. It seems to be her worst day."

"What's wrong with her?" Harding asked.

Dr. Mapes frowned and shook his head. "Frankly, it's got me stumped. There's nothing organically wrong that I can pinpoint, yet she keeps getting worse." He sighed. "There's a lot of things we doctors don't know. But don't tell anybody I said so."

Breakfast over, Harding and Frisco went down to the freight building. Moose Durham's office window had already been boarded up, but their own window was undamaged.

"Guess maybe Durham's willing to call it a draw," Harding said, "At least so far as windows are concerned."

"But nothing else," Frisco commented. "And we won't dare turn our backs on Dobbs or Faraday."

"Or whoever it was that shot Guillford. It's hard watching out for a man when you don't know who he is. I still can't understand about the tracks. Come on, let's take a look inside."

Nothing in the barn appeared to have been touched since Billy had left, and the office was just as they had last seen it. Harding kindled a fire in the stove, and sat down at the desk. Frisco stood close to the stove warming his hands. After a bit he said soberly, "I don't like it, boy. Every time we drive up to Central City we'll be sticking our necks out. You and me are pretty good, if I do say so, but Durham must have a bunch of men working for him. Next time it might not be just Dobbs and Faraday."

"I've been thinking about that," Harding said. "There's four of us now that can drive, once Spud Gagan's back in shape. We've got two wagons."

"But only one work team," Frisco cut in. "And our

saddle horses ain't cut out for pulling.''

"That's right," Harding agreed. "But if we could pick up a couple more horses, we'd be able to bring back two wagon loads at a time. Then there'd be four of us to face whoever Durham sent out to waylay us." He came to an abrupt stop, frowned, and added, "Wait a minute. Maybe we're going about this all wrong."

"Meaning?"

"Well, the stuff all the mines use is about the same: flour, sugar, lard, work clothes, and a few luxuries. Why wouldn't it be a good idea to set up a warehouse right here in Leadville? Then we could make quicker deliveries to the mines, and, more important, pick up additional merchandise when the weather was decent."

"Durham would love that," Frisco said. "He'd likely try to burn us out."

"No more than he would the way things are now," Harding said. "He knows what would happen to his property if he set fire to ours. We could probably make room right here in the barn, if we did a little rearranging."

"It'd cost money," Frisco warned. "Those fellers in Central City would want cash on the barrelhead."

"Well, we've always got the moneybelt. Money's no good except for spending. I think I'll talk it over with Molly."

"You put a lot of store in that girl's knowhow, don't you?"

"That's right," Harding admitted.

"And you think she's something special in other ways," Frisco said. "I saw the way you was looking at her at breakfast."

"A man can look at a pretty girl," Harding said.

"Yeah, even a young man like Billy Gregg. Now *that* would be a match, two smart youngsters about the same age."

"So now you're playing Cupid," Harding said, grinning. "An old goat like you. Well, just so you don't let it interfere with your other duties."

"By the way," Frisco said. "There's something doing today besides church. This is the day the weekly stage comes through from the north. Hetty Cook was reminding me of that last night. It makes one round trip a week. Everybody with nothing better to do watches it arrive. It ought to get here about three this afternoon."

"Maybe we'll join the crowd," Harding said. "Meanwhile, I'm going to the livery stable and see if Abe Wilkins has a couple of work horses for sale. Want to come along?"

"No. I'll stay here where it's warm."

Wilkins did have a work team that he was willing to part with, and after a little haggling, he agreed to a fairly reasonable price. Harding gave him ten dollars to bind the bargain, and got a receipt.

"Something wrong with the horses you've got?" Wilkins asked.

"No, we just want a spare team. Then we can make more trips."

"I get it. You're figuring to take business away from Moose Durham. I saw your notice in the *Courier*. Durham's a hard man to outsmart. I hope you know what you're doing."

"It's worth the gamble," Harding said. "Durham's had things his way too long. I don't like his methods of doing business." He started to leave, then turned back. "Incidentally, where would be the best place to pick up some dynamite and caps, the hardware store?"

"Either there or one of the mines," Wilkins said. He scratched his head. "What do you want with dynamite, if it's any of my business?"

"It isn't," Harding said, and left the barn. Actually, he had no forseeable use for dynamite, but it wouldn't help Durham's nerves to know that he had asked. And Wilkins was sure to pass the word along.

Billy Gregg and Molly Root were among the few who attended church services. The school building was chilly, and the lay preacher not inspiring, but Billy felt a warm glow at being so close to Molly. After church they walked back to the boarding house together, Molly trying to keep the conversation alive. "How did you happen to come to Colorado, Billy?"

"Well, there was four of us boys in the family, and our farm was so small we didn't need all that much help. Me being the youngest, I decided to set out and look for work."

"Did you find any? Before you came with us, I mean?"

"I got a job in Denver," Billy said. "Washing dishes in a restaurant. It seemed like woman's work to me. Besides, Denver is too big. I'm used to small towns. How about you? Were you born here in Leadville?"

"No. I'm from Indiana. My mother died when I was twelve, and Pa and I drifted west. We reached Leadville when I was fifteen. That was four years ago. The next year Pa died of lung fever. I got a job with Mr. Feeney, and I've been there ever since."

"Say, that makes you and me the same age," Billy exclaimed, his shyness temporarily forgotten. "This Mr. Feeney . . . I see his name all over, but I haven't seen him. Is he dead?"

"No, or at least I don't think so," Molly said. "He went away for a spell, and while he was gone, he traded his freighting business for a saloon on the other side of the Divide. Mr. Harding and Mr. Noonan own it now."

"I like them," Billy said. "Don't you?"

"Yes," Molly said. "But I felt a lot more comfortable when Mr. Feeney was here. He didn't stir up trouble."

"And yet somebody wrecked one of his wagons and killed a driver, didn't they?"

"There was never any real proof," Molly said. "The driver was dead when they found him. Of course it's hard to understand. I suppose maybe . . ."

"Yes?"

"Nothing," Molly said, and they turned up the path to Hetty Cook's front door.

Since it was Sunday, Hetty prepared her version of a light noon meal. Stacy Guillford had been home all morning, except for his visit to the doctor's office, and Harding and Frisco had just returned. After the meal, Harding drew Molly aside, and told her his idea about establishing a local supply depot. She wasn't very enthusiastic.

"You'd have to spend a good deal of money. And of course Moose Durham would do everything in his power to hinder you."

"I realize that," Harding said. "Also, we'd have to price things as low as they'd be paying at the new hauling rates. But we could pick our days to drive up to Central City, and in case of trouble, there would be four of us instead of two or three. Provided Spud Gagan gets all right."

"He'll be on the job in the morning. I was talking with his wife at church."

"Good. That settles it. Tomorrow when we deliver the load to the mines I'll talk with some of the operators. They aren't under Durham's thumb, are they?"

"I believe he has an interest in the Dead Indian

106

Mine."

"Then I'll steer clear of that one. It still leaves plenty. What're you planning to do for the rest of the afternoon?"

"Nothing special. I'll probably watch the stage come in. Why?"

"Well, it's a nice day, for a change. Do you ride?"

"Of course. Abe Wilkins has a mare he lets me use."

"Then how about showing me some of the sights hereabouts? All I've seen so far is the Rainbow Mine and the road to Central City."

"Well, I guess so. You'll have to wait for me to change my clothes. I'll just be a minute."

Billy Gregg looked crestfallen when Harding and Molly left the house, and Frisco tried to cheer him up. "They'll be back, son. You've got nothing to worry about."

"Who's worrying?"

Frisco shrugged and said, "Likely there's a checkerboard around here. Are you a checker player?"

"No, thanks. I think I'll go down to the barn. See you at supper."

"Sure," Frisco said, and shook his head. Being young and in love must be pretty tough.

Harding and Molly timed their ride so as to get back for the stage arrival. They returned Molly's mare to the livery stable, and walked Harding's sorrel to their own barn. Billy Gregg was in the office. He had found a broom, and was sweeping up. He seemed relieved to see them.

"Thought I might as well keep busy. I'm not used to loafing."

"This is Sunday," Molly reminded him. "You don't have to work all the time. Why don't you come with us to watch the stage arrive?"

"Sure," Billy said, and put up the broom.

The stage was a few minutes late, which Molly said was not unusual. Harding noticed Dobbs and Faraday with their backs against the stage depot. If they saw him, they gave no sign. He turned his attention to the stagecoach as it rattled to a stop, swaying on its straps.

The first passenger out was an elderly lady, well muffled against the cold. An equally old man moved up to welcome her. Harding was watching them when Billy tugged at his sleeve.

"It's him!"

Harding swung his eyes back to the coach. Just stepping down was a man he had seen once before, but had never expected to see again.

"Who is he?" Molly asked.

Harding turned to look at her. "Remember the crooked card dealer in Central City we told you about? The man who tried to cheat Billy? He's the one in the black coat. Dammit, if he had to leave Central City why couldn't he have gone to some place other than Leadville?"

"That's all we need," Molly said. "Somebody else gunning for you." She shivered. "Let's get back to Mrs. Cook's."

Seeing the crooked gambler had made Harding uneasy. A man like that wouldn't hesitate to shoot you in the back. The thought kept preying on him, and about nine o'clock, when the rest of the household was thinking of going to bed, Harding decided to take a turn up and down the main street, hoping he might find the fellow and get it over with. The only places open were the saloons. When Harding failed to find him, he decided to give it up until later. He started back toward the boarding house.

108

Chapter Fifteen

Rex Fargo, the crooked gambler who had come so close to separating Billy Gregg from his savings in Central City, had been dismayed at the sight of Harding and his friends watching the stage unload. Trained by his profession not to show emotion, he had kept a poker face, and pretended not to notice them as he carried his carpetbag to the hotel, where he registered under his true name. Well, not exactly true; the name given him at birth had been discarded some time before, when he had fled the East two jumps ahead of a posse.

In the privacy of his hotel room, Fargo gave vent to his anger. He had never again expected to see the man who had unmasked him in Central City, thereby putting an end to a lucrative, albeit dishonest, business. Fate had played him a dirty trick in bringing him and his nemesis to the same town. Once the man started talking, no one in Leadville would touch Fargo's game with a ten-foot pole. No two ways about it, he would have to move on to some place where his reputation was unknown. Unless . . . He sat on the edge of the bed and put his mind to work.

It was full dark when Fargo went down to the hotel dining room, which consisted of one family-sized table and four stools at a short counter. Except for himself and the man in charge, the same one who had signed him in, the place was unoccupied. Fargo found out why, when he tasted the tough beef and lumpy potatoes. He made no comment on the quality of the food, but said instead, "I noticed a man at the stage depot who looked familiar. Tall, dark, and wearing city clothes."

"That would likely be the newcomer, Harding," the hotelman said. "Is he a friend of yours?"

"Harding?" Fargo repeated, shaking his head. "No. The man I mistook him for is named Nolan. Come to think of it, he'd look older now. It's been half a dozen years since I saw him. Is there a good saloon in town?"

"Depends on what kind you're looking for," the hotelman said. "There are three of them: the Mexicali, which, as you might guess, is patronized mostly by Mexicans; the Fast Buck, where most of the local businessmen go; and the Ace of Spades."

Fargo looked at him inquiringly. "I notice you didn't say anything about the third one. Is there something wrong with it?"

"Not at all," the hotelman said quickly. "In fact it belongs to Moose Durham, who owns most of this hotel. It's just that things get a little rough down there now and then. Of course if you're looking for excitement, the Ace of Spades is the place to go."

"No, thanks," Fargo said, smiling. "After that stagecoach ride all I want is about ten hours sleep. See you in the morning."

"Sure," the hotelman said. "Pleasant dreams." As he watched Fargo go up to the second floor, he wondered what this stranger was doing in Leadville, but since the information hadn't been volunteered, he wasn't about to ask. A man could get into a heap of trouble sticking his nose into other folks' affairs.

Fargo made all the sounds associated with getting ready for bed, including dropping his shoes on the floor, then blew out the lamp and waited impatiently until the hotelman came up stairs, clomped down the hallway, and presumably entered his own room. After a

110

prudent interval, Fargo went downstairs in his stocking feet, stopped to put on his shoes in the small lobby, and left the hotel, closing the door quietly behind him. Keeping to the shadows, he made his way to a spot from which he could look across the street into the windows of the Ace of Spades saloon.

The place was well patronized for a Sunday, when many of its customers would probably be recuperating from a Saturday night hangover. As the hotelman had intimated, there was a rough-looking bunch at the bar. Two of the men, who seemed to be together, looked especially formidable. Fargo singled them out for his particular attention, and when they left the saloon, weaving a little, he cut across the street to intercept them.

They turned to look at him, and then he said mildly, "Excuse me, but would you gentlemen be interested in picking up a little easy money?"

The two men stared at him suspiciously, and for a moment Fargo was afraid he had chosen a bad time to make his approach. Both were big and burly; if they were in a truculent mood, they could tear him to pieces. However, after exchanging a glance with his partner, one of them demanded, "Doing what? And who the hell are you, anyway. I ain't ever seen you before."

"Who I am doesn't make much difference," Fargo said, keeping the tremor out of his voice. "And as for what I want you to do, you'd probably do it for free when you find out. If you don't like for a decent woman to be taken advantage of, that is."

This obviously intrigued them, for one of them said, "Let's have it straight, mister. What woman are you talking about?"

"My sister," Fargo said, knowing he had them hooked. "As fine a girl as ever lived, God rest her soul."

"She's dead?"

"Two weeks now," Fargo said solemnly. "Dead by her own hand, and all on account of a smooth-talking bastard who's right here in Leadville." He lowered his voice and added, "Fellow who calls himself Harding. Let me tell you what he did."

Their interest fully captured, Fargo went on with the story he had concocted in his hotel room. A naturally glib talker, he made it sound very convincing. By the time he had finished, the two strangers were as outraged as he had meant for them to be. In fact they would have refused Fargo's money, but he insisted on giving each of them a couple of silver dollars.

"Handle it your own way, men, but make it soon. The sooner the better, or he may skip out on you."

"Sure," one of them said, then, after a brief hesitation, "There's just one thing. We ain't going to kill him. I'm not taking a chance on a hangman's noose."

"Of course not," Fargo said. "All I want is for Harding to get a lesson on what happens when you mistreat an innocent girl. If he's foolish enough to go to the law, which I doubt, you can tell him why you did it. Leaving me out, of course. Once word gets around, he'll have to hightail it out of Leadville before he gets ridden out on a rail. You've got nothing to worry about. Oh, by the way, don't give him a chance to go for his gun. He'd as soon shoot an unarmed man as look at him. Good luck."

Half an hour later, as Harding passed the alley between the hardware store and the feed store on his way back to Mrs. Cook's, he heard a faint noise from the darkness. Before he could react, something crashed down on his head, and everything went black.

Some time later, he was jolted back to consciousness by cold water being thrown on his face. He jerked to a sitting position, and groaned involuntarily at the pain in his head. A man laughed, and said harshly, "Stand up, mister!" Then, before Harding could comply, he was yanked to his feet. His hand went automatically to his holster, which he found empty. Again the coarse laugh, then a fist caught him on the cheek, knocking him down again.

Although he had no idea what it was all about, Harding had the presence of mind to feign unconsciousness. Lying motionless except for his eyes, he saw that he was under the starlit sky, with no sign of buildings nearby. Obviously he had been out long enough to be moved away from the center of town. His mind began to clear, and he said as calmly as he could, "Before this goes any farther, would somebody mind telling me what you're trying to prove?"

"Don't play dumb!" one of the men growled. "We know all about you and that girl in Denver." He kicked Harding in the ribs. "Do you want to stand up and fight like a man, or would you rather have your brains kicked out?"

Outnumbered though he was, and hurting from the blow to his head and the kick in his ribs, Harding knew that he had no choice but to fight. He started to get up, moving more slowly than necessary, then suddenly rose to his feet and swung a haymaker which caught one of the men flush on the nose. Blood spurted and the man cursed, but before Harding could follow up his advantage, the other man caught him from the rear, pinning his arms to his sides. The one with the bloody nose drew back his fist, and Harding braced himself. Then a gun spoke, and Marshal Banks called sharply, "Break it up! I'll put a slug through the first man that moves. You, there, let loose of Harding's arms.''

Reluctantly, the one holding Harding let him go. Harding turned to face the marshal, whose sixgun was clearly visible in the pale moonlight.

"You got here just in time, Marshal. These two baboons were about to kill me.''

"That ain't so,'' one of the men muttered. "We just aimed to show you what we think of a skunk who would drive a decent woman to kill herself.''

Puzzled, Harding asked, "What woman? What the devil are you talking about?''

There was a moment's hesitation, then the bloody nosed man said uncertainly, "From what he told us . . .'' He let the sentence hang, and turned to his companion. "Do you reckon we've been played for suckers?''

Before he could be answered, Marshal Banks said curtly, "Whatever it is, this is no place to thrash it out.'' He stooped to pick up Harding's gun from the dirt, thrust it in his own belt, and continued, "We're all going to my office. When I talk to someone, I like to be able to see what he looks like.''

Single file, with the two thugs in front, followed by Harding, and then the marshal, they returned to the main street and entered Banks' office, where a lamp was already glowing. Banks squinted at them in the yellow light.

"You two work for Hortense at the Consolidated, don't you? If I was to lock you up, I suppose she'd be here first thing in the morning to bail you out.''

"Now hold on, Marshal,'' Bloody Nose protested. "We ain't . . .''

"Don't talk until I tell you to,'' Banks snapped. He turned to face Harding. "Let's hear your version of the affair first.''

114

Harding smiled ruefully.

"I'm afraid I can't explain anything, Marshal. I was walking along the main street when somebody hit me over the head and knocked me out. When I came to, these handsome rascals had dragged me to where you just found us, and were about to beat me up. One of them said something about a girl in Denver. That's all that was said, and before I could ask any questions, the fracas started. Maybe you'll have better luck than I did at getting an explanation."

"Oh, I'll get one, all right," Banks said. He pointed a finger at the man Harding had hit, whose nose had stopped bleeding. "You tell me about it, and stick to the truth. You're not smart enough to make up a convincing lie."

"All right, Marshal," the man said, looking thoroughly deflated. "This feller came up to us after the saloon, and . . ."

"Just a minute. *What* feller? Do you mean Harding?"

"No, it was somebody else. He didn't give us his name. Sort of on the small side, and he talked like a dude. Anyway, he told us how this feller here . . ." He pointed at Harding. "How he messed around with this girl in Denver. The dude's sister, she was. Anyway, she up and killed herself. He asked my friend and me to teach Harding a lesson. We waited—"

The marshal motioned for silence, and peered intently toward the doorway.

"Thought I heard something out there, but I guess it was just a cat. Go on."

"There ain't much more to tell, Marshal. We was about to do what we was paid . . . what he asked us to do, when you showed up."

Harding stepped quickly to the doorway, and was in

115

time to see someone dart into the hotel. He turned back to find the marshal half out of his chair, his pistol in his hand.

"I wasn't going to run," Harding said. "But I think I can tell you who tricked these gents into waylaying me. If you hurry, you'll probably catch him in the hotel."

"Suppose you let me handle this my way," Banks said irritably. "Just to keep things straight, though, who were you going to accuse?"

"I never heard his name," Harding said. "But he came in on today's stagecoach. The only other time I've seen him was in Central City, where he was dealing a crooked hand of poker. He wasn't too happy when I called him on it. As for his having a sister, I wouldn't know about that, but he has good reason to hate my guts. It's at least worth investigating, don't you think?"

The marshal nodded and rose to his feet.

"You and me, Harding, are going over to the hotel." He gestured at the other two. "You boys will stay here, and just to make sure you don't get other ideas, I'll lock you in a cell. Get moving!"

Without protesting, the two men entered a cell. Banks locked them in, pocketed the key, and motioned for Harding to come with him. They crossed the street and entered the hotel. In response to the marshal's yell, the hotelman came downstairs, his night shirt tucked into his pants.

"What's up, Marshal?"

"You got a man staying here?" Banks asked. "Feller who came in on today's stage?"

"Yes, sir, he's up in room six. Do you want me to roust him out?"

As he spoke, there was the clatter of hoofs in the street. Harding looked quickly at the marshal.

"I've got a hunch that's your man, Marshal, leaving

town in a hurry, most likely on a stolen horse. He was probably listening outside your office. Remember you thought you heard a noise?''

The marshal went up the stairs two at a time. There was the sound of a door being opened, then he came running down.

"The room's empty, all right, and the bed ain't been slept in. Damnit, I'll have a time catching him, with this much head start. I'll go saddle my horse.''

"Mind if I make a suggestion?'' Harding asked. "Why don't you just let him go? There's not much chance he'll ever come back, not after tipping his hand by running away. And stealing a horse at that.''

"You don't want him caught?'' the marshal exclaimed, and Harding shook his head.

"So far as I'm concerned, it's a closed book.''

"How about the fellers he hired to beat you up?''

Harding grinned. "No hard feeling there, either. I figure we came out about even. I've got a sore head, and one of them has a smashed nose. If you'll turn them loose, and give me my gun back, we'll call it a draw.''

"I'll be damned,'' the marshal said. "If you ain't a funny one. All right, if you don't want to make a complaint, I'll turn 'em loose.''

"And I'll go home and go to bed,'' Harding said. "After you give me back my gun, that is.''

The marshal handed it over, and Harding left the hotel and headed for the boarding house, pausing long enough to recover his hat, which had fallen off when he had been attacked. He'd have a time explaining to Frisco how it had gotten so dirty.

Chapter Sixteen

Monday morning Spud Gagan was waiting in front of the barn when Harding and his two companions came from breakfast. After being introduced to Billy Gregg, and shaking hands all around, he said curiously, "I couldn't figure why there was smoke coming from the stovepipe and nobody here. Someone's fixed the big door so I couldn't open it. What's been going on?"

"Quite a bit," Molly said. "Some of it you wouldn't believe. How are you feeling?"

"Pretty good," Gagan said. "A little stiff, but that'll wear off in a day or so."

Harding had been unlocking the door, and they all filed into the barn. Inside the office, Molly said to Gagan, "Mr. Feeney doesn't own the business any more. It belongs to Mr. Harding and Mr. Noonan."

"The devil you say! What happened to Feeney?"

"We made a swap," Harding said. "I'll tell you about it later. Along with the other things that have happened. Meanwhile, we've got a load of supplies to deliver to a mine. Why don't you and I do it, and on the way I'll fill you in on what you don't know." He turned to Molly. "It goes to Consolidated, doesn't it?"

"That's right. Spud can show you where it is."

"Fair enough. Frisco, you and Billy could be cleaning out a couple of stalls and getting the wagon ready. Molly, will you go to Dr. Mapes's and get five hundred dollars out of the moneybelt?"

"Aren't you taking a chance?" Molly asked. "I could go a long way on five hundred dollars."

Harding grinned. "Why stop at five hundred? You could have taken the whole lot, but you're too darned honest. Otherwise we wouldn't have trusted you in the first place."

Consolidated was on the same road as Rainbow, but three miles farther along. Gagan drove the wagon, and Harding kept a sharp lookout for trouble, while he brought Gagan up to date.

"Dobbs and Faraday are pretty sore, after the way their plan fizzled. And of course Dobbs remembers the fight we had in the Mexicali. But they don't worry me as much as the fellow who shot Guillford. Dobbs and Faraday I know, and can watch out for. The other man could be a total stranger. I keep thinking about how he brushed out his tracks. It doesn't make sense unless there was something about them that was unusual, like maybe being made by a woman."

"Or by a man with only one leg," Gagan said, and Harding looked at him sharply.

"What're you driving at?"

"Well, Durham's strawboss at the freight yard has a peg leg. His name is Ike Langhorn, and he's pure poison. Fast as lightning with a sixgun. But if it was him, I can't see how he'd miss."

"I heard him cock his gun," Harding said. "It must be an old single action. It gave us time to duck. You know you may have hit it. A peg leg would certainly make a distinctive print. It's funny the marshal didn't notice it when he first looked."

"If he did, he would've kept it to himself. Marshal Banks ain't about to tangle with Ike Langhorn. Or with Moose Durham, either."

"I'll let it ride for the time being," Harding said. "See what you think of my idea for a local warehouse."

Gagan listened attentively as Harding outlined his

plan. When he finished, Gagan said positively, "It won't work."

"No? Why not?"

"Well, you're the boss and everything, but I've been around Leadville longer than you have. Like Molly told you, Durham don't control the mines, except for the Dead Indian. But he's hauled a lot of freight from those outfits in Central City. If he told them that selling to you would mean losing his business, they'd listen."

Harding hadn't thought of that, and said so. It temporarily set him back on his heels. Then he asked, "How do the suppliers in Central City get their stuff?"

"By short line from Denver."

"In that case, we'll have to go over their heads and order direct. We can pick up the stuff at the depot in Central City."

"Do you think the Denver outfits will go along with it?"

"I can't be sure about that," Harding conceded. "But neither can the Central City suppliers. I don't suppose Durham's influence goes as far as Denver?"

"No, I wouldn't think so."

"Then maybe we can bluff the firms in Central City. They won't want to get cut out of any business. For all they know, Frisco and I might be well financed."

"I wish you luck," Gagan said, and pointed with the whip. "There's Consolidated, right over the next rise. I might as well warn you to be braced for a surprise. Oh yes, the manager's name is Blivens."

Gagan guided the wagon to the unloading dock, and Harding stepped down and went back to the door marked office. Inside, there was a very large, lantern-jawed woman seated at a desk. She looked up and asked, "What'll it be, sonny?"

"I'm looking for Mr. Blivens."

120

"You've come to the wrong place. He's down below."

"You mean he's in the mine?"

"No, a lot deeper than that. If there's a hell, he's in it."

Mystified, he could only stare at her.

"What's the matter, sonny? Ain't you ever heard of hell before? I've been through it a dozen times, thanks to that old buzzard I was married to, may he rest in brimstone."

"You mean you're Mrs. Blivens?"

"Don't call me 'Missus.' I'm Hortense to my friends, and poison to my enemies. But if you mean was the old devil my husband, the answer is yes. Now quit wasting my time and get down to business, if you've got any."

"Yes'm," Harding said. In spite of Hortense Blivens's crustiness, he found her refreshing. "I'm Allan Harding, one of the new owners of Feeney Freight Lines. We've got a load of supplies at your dock."

"Well, why didn't you say so?"

"Begging your pardon, but you haven't given me much chance."

"Now don't get smart-alecky!" Hortense said. "I suppose you want your money. Let me tell you something, Mr. New Owner Harding, I saw your ad in the *Courier*, and if you think I'm going to pay full price for the hauling, you're off your noggin'."

"You're entitled to the same rates as anybody else," Harding said. "Even though you gave us the order before the rates went down. Is anything else bothering you?"

"Nothing bothers me," Hortense said. "Except handsome strangers all the time pestering me to marry them." For the first time, she smiled, and Harding relaxed. "Give me your bill and I'll pay it, at the new low rates." She rose heavily, and moved up to the counter separating her office space from the rest of the room. Her eyes, an unusual shade of blue, were on a level with Harding's.

Harding laid the bill on the counter. "I imagine you'll want someone to check the load before you pay for it."

"Ain't necessary," she said. "If there's anything missing I'll take it out of your hide." She reached under the counter and came up with a horse pistol, which she was nice enough not to point at Harding. "I'm just a poor helpless widow, but I aim to take care of myself."

"I bet you do," Harding said, grinning. "Have you got a minute to talk?"

"If you've got anything worth talking about," she said. "I'll stop you when it gets boring."

"How would you like to get your supplies right out of Leadville, instead of all the way from Central City?"

"Keep talking."

"Well, my partner and I plan on stocking a warehouse in town. We'll try to keep enough staples on hand to supply our customers. Of course the stuff will have to come from Central City originally, but not on special order."

Hortense Blivens looked at him narrowly. "Will this put that Root girl out of a job? I mean you and your partner taking over."

"By no means," Harding said. "We even offered to make her a partner, but she turned it down."

"Smart girl."

"What do you mean by that?"

"She'd be climbing aboard a sinking ship. Moose Durham ain't going to let you get away with it."

"Are you afraid of Durham?"

"Sonny, I ain't afraid of anything that wears pants, Moose Durham included. And you can tell him I said

122

so."

"Then you'll buy from us when we get set up?"

"I'll buy from whoever gives me the best deal. I might even shade it a little in your favor."

"I'm flattered."

"You needn't be. It's just that I like Molly Root. But don't tell her I said so."

"No, Mrs. Blivens."

"And don't call me Mrs. Blivens. I'm Hortense. Here's your money."

Returning to the wagon, which was being unloaded by a couple of burly Consolidated men, Harding said wryly, "Why didn't you tell me Blivens was a woman?"

"Tell the truth, I ain't rightly sure she is. She looks like a woman, and claims to be one, but I'd hate to tangle with her. How did she strike you?"

"I liked her," Harding said. "Even though she did keep calling me 'sonny.' Another thing, she agreed to deal with us if we get our warehouse set up."

"You must've made a hit with her."

"No, the truth is she's doing it mostly for Molly. Speaking of whom, we'd better get back to the barn."

Frisco and Billy had cleaned out two of the stalls and were greasing the wheels of the formerly unused wagon. Harding looked it over, nodded his approval, and went into the office, where Molly glanced up from her desk and asked, "How did it go? Did anything unusual happen?"

"You know blamed well what happened. I walked in on Mrs.—excuse me, on Hortence Blivens, and got the surprise of my life. Did you and Gagan cook this up between you?"

"We thought the shock would do you good," Molly said. "What did you think of Hortense?"

"She's a lot of woman," Harding said. "Incidentally, or not so incidentally, she wouldn't agree to do business with us until she was sure you were still here. I can't tell you she likes you, because she ordered me not to."

"Do business? You mean she's going to be a customer?"

"That's what she said, and she doesn't look like the kind of person to change her mind easily. But one swallow doesn't make a spring, as the saying goes. Do we have any more orders to pick up?"

"Not until Wednesday, which means going to Central City tomorrow."

"Then I think I'll visit some more of the mines and try to win them over to our new plan. Say, why don't you come along? They'd trust you before they would me. Unless you think you'd be sticking your neck out too far."

Molly smiled. "If you men are willing to risk being shot at, I'm game to take a chance. I'll go get Abe Wilkins's mare."

"I'll go with you, but first let me say something to Frisco." He went out into the barn.

"How does it look, partner?"

Frisco shrugged. "The wagon's okay, and the horses drive well enough. I understand we've got us a customer."

"Yes. A real pretty lady named Hortense. Wait till you meet her."

"Oh no you don't! Gagan described her to me. What do we do next?"

"Molly and I are going to call on a few of the mines. Tomorrow we'll take both wagons to Central City. Don't worry, it's warming up. There's a load to bring back, and we can fill the other wagon for stock for our warehouse." He glanced around and pointed at one corner of the barn. "There's enough room right here for a start. You and Billy pick up some lumber, and build a few shelves. There's a lumber yard half a mile east, just off the north end of the main street. Molly showed it to me yesterday on our ride."

"All right, we'll take care of it. Won't we, Billy?"

"Sure," Billy said. His usual smile was missing, and Harding thought he knew why. Well, there would be other times when the boy could go riding with Molly. Harding looked at Frisco.

"By the way, did Gagan tell you about the peg-legged man, and a possible explanation for those brushed-out tracks?"

"He told me. Langhorn did it."

Harding nodded. "So he's another one we'll have to watch out for. We're getting quite a collection: Dobbs, Faraday, maybe even Moose Durham himself, who has probably done some killing. That's assuming the crooked gambler doesn't come back."

"Well, at least we can't complain of being bored," Frisco said, grinning. "You know something, I'm beginning to be glad we came. Good luck."

"The same to you," Harding said. He crossed over to Spud Gagan, who was inspecting the shoes on the newly bought horses.

"Are you up to driving to Central City tomorrow?"

"Sure thing, boss," Gagan said. "I heal fast. But about this plan of yours to set up a warehouse in Leadville. I suppose you know it's going to be risky."

"You mean on account of Moose Durham?"

"Mostly," Gagan said. "You may end up with a barn full of merchandise, and nobody with guts enough to trade with you."

"Then we'll sell all the stuff to Hortense," Harding said, slapping Gagan on the shoulder. "All my life I've

125

been taking chances. So has Frisco. This is just one more."

"Yeah," Gagan said. "Well, it's your funeral."

"I wish you hadn't said that," Harding told him, grinning. "You take it easy the rest of the day so you'll be rested for tomorrow." And he joined Molly to go to the livery barn.

Chapter Seventeen

With Molly acting as pilot, she and Harding visited the mines she thought might be most likely to accept his proposition. They met a mixed reception. The first mine operator, a stubborn man by the name of Mulholland, turned them down flat. He was leery of anything or anybody new. Harding mentally scratched him off the list.

Two others agreed to "think about it," which was somewhat better than an outright refusal. The fourth, an Irishman named Casey, was enthusiastic about the idea.

"I never did like having to order so far in advance. You can count on Shamrock Mine if you get the plan working."

Riding back to town, Harding said, "Well, one yes and two maybes isn't bad. You know, I think you are mainly responsible. None of them would have listened to a stranger."

"Thanks," Molly said. "But I believe you would have talked them into it. You can be pretty persuasive when you try."

"The important thing is whether we can deliver. That depends a lot on my reception in Central City. If I flop there, I'll take the short line to Denver and talk to the wholesalers."

"I envy you," Molly said. "Not the part about arguing with the suppliers, but going to Denver. I haven't been there since Pa and I came through four years ago."

"Well, I wish I could take you with me, but that

would set the town on its ear. Maybe we can make it later, with Hetty Cook as chaperone. Or you can go there on your honeymoon.''

Molly shook her head. "No honeymoons for me. I'll end up an old maid, knitting by the fire.''

"We'll see," Harding said, trying vainly to picture Molly in that role.

They reached Leadville, and both of them noticed that the glass had been replaced in Durham's office window. As Harding led his sorrel from the livery stable after returning the mare, he caught a glimpse of Durham at his desk. The light was too bad for him to see Durham's expression.

Frisco and Billy, with help from Gagan, had put together some serviceable shelving. Molly and Harding admired their handiwork, then went into the office. Harding asked, "Do you keep copies of all the pickup orders?''

"That's right.''

"Suppose you make a list of the items most frequently ordered. Not over two hundred dollars worth if you can help it. All I'm taking with me is that five hundred you got from Dr. Mapes.''

Molly smiled.

"I won't need to refer to the orders. I've written so many of them I could do it in my sleep.''

"Good. I'm going to talk to Frisco.''

Across the street, Moose Durham was conversing with Ike Langhorn, who hadn't been visible through the window.

"I wish I knew what the hell Harding's got in mind.''

"Why don't you ask him?'' Langhorn suggested ironically.

"This is nothing to joke about, dammit. I don't know what makes Harding tick. I've been trying to run his outfit out of business, and so far he's done a pretty good job of stopping me, thanks in part to Dobbs and Faraday letting themselves be outsmarted. Another thing, he and that Root girl have been out together all afternoon. I'd like to know what they're cooking up."

"Want me to do some scouting around?"

"No," Durham said. "I've got a more important job for you. I happen to know they're picking up a load in Central City Wednesday, which means they'll drive up tomorrow. I want you to get there ahead of them and see what they do. You'll have to get an early start."

"Who'll watch the barn?"

"Faraday can fill in for you. He's smarter than Dobbs. My main reason for sending you is that Harding doesn't know what you look like."

"Gagan does."

"Yes, but I doubt if Gagan will make the drive. It'll probably be Harding and his partner, and maybe the kid."

"Do I make trouble for them?"

"Not this time. That'll come later, after I know what they're up to."

Langhorn left Durham's office by way of the back door. He welcomed the chance to get away from the barn, even though it meant a long ride. Secretly, in spite of Durham's instructions, he hoped he could get another crack at Harding. It rankled him that he had botched the first attempt. If he eliminated Harding, Moose would overlook his insubordination.

At sunup the next day, Langhorn was on his way, riding a dun gelding. He used a saddle with a special stirrup to accommodate his peg leg.

Half an hour later, the two Feeney wagons set out, Gagan driving the first, with Billy at his side, Frisco and Harding on the second. Harding's saddle horse was tied to the tailgate in case he should need it.

Most of the snow had evaporated or soaked into the ground, and it was starting out like a pleasant day. There were a few patches of snow left, however, and Frisco pointed to a set of fresh hoof prints.

"Looks like we ain't the only early birds."

"No," Harding said. "But there's been only one horse by here, so it wouldn't be both Dobbs and Faraday, and I have an idea they work as a team. Just to be safe, though, I'll get in the saddle and scout ahead."

His precautions proved to be unnecessary, and at about six o'clock they reached Central City. Remembering what had happened on the previous trip, Harding rode immediately to the supply house, where the same man he had talked to before was getting ready to close down for the night.

"Is our load ready for tomorrow morning?"

"Yes, sir, it sure is. I don't generally get bamboozled twice."

"Good. Have you got a minute to talk?"

"Well, it's supper time. Will you take long?"

"No. First, though, are you the boss?"

"I like to think so. Why?"

"I want to pick up an extra load of merchandise. My partner and I are planning on carrying some goods in stock at Leadville, where they'll be handier to the mines, especially when the road is blocked by snow."

"Well, I don't know," the man said. "I like it the way it's been. Don't see any point in changing."

"You wouldn't be afraid of Moose Durham, would you?"

"Yes, confound it! He hauls twice as much as your

outfit does."

"Well, at least sleep on it," Harding requested. "And remember, we'll be paying cash, if that's what bothers you. I'll see you first thing in the morning. Good night."

"Night," the man said, and closed the door.

Harding rode to the stable they had patronized before, and this time he received a more cordial greeting.

"Harding, ain't it? Do you want to put up your horse overnight?"

"Yes, and two teams and wagons. They'll be along after a bit."

"Two, huh? Ain't that a little unusual?"

"It won't be, from now on," Harding said, and added to himself, "I hope."

By the time Harding had his horse stripped, the two wagons arrived. Frisco looked at the stable man as though he were something which had just crawled out from under a rock, but he kept his thoughts to himself. All four of them went to the restaurant and sat at the counter. Harding grinned at Billy.

"Do you feel like going back to that saloon and playing a little five-card stud?"

"Not on your life!" Billy said. "But I wouldn't mind looking around before we go to the hotel. This town has Leadville beat a mile."

"I'll go with you," Frisco offered. "My rear end feels like it's paralyzed."

"I guess we could all stand to stretch our legs," Harding said. "Gagan?"

Spud shook his head. "A bed would look mighty good to me right now, if nobody has any objections."

"Go right ahead. We might as well stay at the Colorado. You can rent us a couple of rooms."

After the meal, Gagan went to the hotel, and the other three sauntered along the main street, where most businesses were just closing for the night. They went into a saloon, not the one where Billy had been fleeced, and had a drink, Billy taking beer. By then all of them were sleepy, and they went to the hotel. Billy shared a room with Gagan, who was already snoring, and the other two took one on the opposite side of the hall, facing out over the street. They were about to turn in when Harding motioned for silence.

"Hear that?"

"Hear *what*?" Frisco asked.

"Somebody walking past under our window."

"Well, it's a public sidewalk," Frisco said. "So what's so special about it?"

"It sounded like a man with a peg leg," Harding told him. "Either that or a crutch. I'll be back." He left the room and hurried downstairs.

There were four men in sight, none of them with a peg leg. Harding returned to the room.

"Guess I was imagining things. Let's go to bed."

Out in the street, Ike Langhorn stepped from between two buildings. For just a minute he had considered gunning Harding down, but he had held himself in check. At least four men had seen him walk by, and would identify him by his wooden leg. For all he knew, one of them might be a lawman. And it was six blocks to the stable where he had left his horse.

Morning came, and after breakfast Harding went to the supply house, where he found the same man on duty. The fellow's expression didn't look encouraging, and his first words bore out that impression.

"I slept on it, like you asked me to, but it's no go. All my orders will have to come from the mines."

"If that's your decision, I'll have to accept it,"

Harding said, hiding his disappointment. "Of course it'll just make things tougher for all of us."

"How do you figure?"

"Well, I'll have to buy direct from the wholesalers in Denver. I doubt if anybody will try to prevent me from picking up goods at the railroad depot. One of our wagons will be along in a few minutes for the regular pickup. It'll likely be our last."

"Now wait a minute, mister! Where does that leave me?"

"You'll still have Rocky Mountain's business," Harding said cheerfully. "Unless Durham decides to do as we do. He might cut out the middleman's profit, too. Well, here comes our wagon."

Frisco and Gagan were on the seat, with Billy walking alongside. Gagan backed the wagon up against the dock, and a man they hadn't seen before came out to help with the loading. Frisco got off the wagon, and Harding drew him aside.

"I didn't get anywhere with my proposition, so I'm going to take the train to Denver and talk to some wholesalers."

"Want me to come along?"

"No. I'll feel safer with the three of you guarding the load. You can ride my sorrel. If my trip to Denver pans out I'll be driving the other wagon back with a full load. I don't really expect anybody to give you trouble, and they surely won't be expecting me to be bringing in another load, so we both ought to make it all right. If we don't, well, that's something that can't be helped."

"When does the train leave?"

"I'm going over to the depot now and find out. It's somewhere around nine or ten this morning. The livery stable man told me that much. If I don't see you again before you leave, good luck."

"We'll make out," Frisco said, and went back to the wagon.

Ike Langhorn, who had been watching from a safe distance, followed Harding far enough to see him enter the depot. Since the line ran only to Denver, and there was just one train a day, he could guess Harding's intentions. When the train pulled out an hour later, Langhorn was riding in the caboose.

Chapter Eighteen

The train was slow and jerky, due no doubt to an uneven roadbed. Soot and cinders seeped in around the edges of the windows. To add to the discomfort, there was a woman aboard with two youngsters who ran up and down the aisle, and a squalling baby in her lap. Harding felt sorry for her, but it didn't add to his enjoyment of the trip, and when the train ground to a stop he was glad to get off.

Denver was not a strange town to him, so he had no difficulty finding the wholesale district. He picked what seemed to be the largest and busiest store, and asked to see the manager. After a brief wait in a stuffy anteroom, he was told to go in.

Seated at a cluttered desk was a thin faced man with his shirt sleeves rolled up. He motioned Harding to a chair, and said curtly, "As you can see, I'm pretty busy, so please come right to the point."

"Glad to," Harding said. "In the first place, my name is Allan Harding."

"Lucius Gibbs," the thin faced man said, not offering to shake hands.

"I'm from Leadville, and one of the new owners of Feeney Freight Lines. Does that name mean anything to you?"

"It does. We've shipped a number of orders care of Feeney. You say you're the new owner.?"

"Along with my partner, Frisco Noonan. You said to get to the point. We're setting up a warehouse in Leadville, and would like to buy from you direct. At wholesale prices, of course."

Gibbs began to show a little interest.

"What do the mine operators think of this idea?"

"I've talked to four of them. No, five, counting Rainbow, and had only one definite rejection. And of course any of the mines that don't switch over can continue to buy direct. We'll haul their goods as in the past."

Gibbs tilted back in his chair and laced his fingers together behind his head.

"I've heard something about a rate war on the Central City-Leadville run. Is that your doing?"

"No," Harding said. "The Rocky Mountain Freighting Company started it. We just lowered our rates in order to be competitive. Incidentally, I put this proposition to the supply house in Central City and was turned down. They're afraid of antagonizing Moose Durham, of Rocky Mountain. If you share their fear, I won't take up any more of your time."

"Durham is just a name to me. But you aren't even that much, or weren't until five minutes ago. Do you have any local references?"

"I have this," Harding said, and laid some currency on the desk. "I can also give you the names of some local men you might want to call. I was in business here once."

"Nothing beats cash," Gibbs said, smiling for the first time. "Let me get this straight. You want to buy from us and resell to the mines. What's the point, more profit?"

"Partly," Harding said, relaxing. "I have no objections to making money. But it will also allow us to supply the mines when the road is blocked by snow or landslides. We can choose our own times to pick up the stuff at Central City."

Gibbs nodded. "All right, I see nothing wrong with the idea in theory. Do you have an order for us now?"

Harding handed over the list Molly had prepared.

"Have someone total it up, and I'll pay you right now. Future orders can be sent C.O.D. Could this stuff go out on tomorrow's train?"

"Just a minute," Gibbs said, and went to a connecting door. He spoke to someone Harding couldn't see.

"Can we ship this by tomorrow?"

There was a brief pause, then a man's voice answered, "Yes, Mr. Gibbs."

"Good. Get going on it." He closed the door and turned back to face Harding.

"Anything else on your mind?"

"No," Harding said. "When do you want your money?"

"Tomorrow morning will do. Say about eight o'clock. The train leaves at nine-thirty."

Feeling elated, Harding left the office and the building. He went to a restaurant which he had patronized in the past, had a good meal, and headed for the Ames Hotel, where he planned to spend the night.

Larimer Street was far busier than he remembered it. Heavy wagons raised a cloud of dust, their drivers cursing each other good naturedly. Dozens of pedestrians were on the sidewalk, everyone seeming to be in a hurry.

The Ames was on a quieter side street, which was why Harding had chosen it. There was little foot traffic here, and after a bit he tensed as he heard the distinctive footsteps which he associated with a peg leg. Without turning to look back, he cut across the street toward a pawnshop. Pretending to be interested in something in the window, he saw the reflection of the man who had

137

been behind him. He was a complete stranger, but as Harding had surmised, he had a peg leg. Harding started to turn and face him, at the same time moving his hand toward his gun. Before he could complete the turn, the man across the street drew his own gun and fired, the bullet striking Harding in the side and knocking him down. He managed to turn his head in time to see the man he was sure was Langhorn duck into a store building.

A chubby little man came rushing out of the pawn shop, his shoes crunching broken glass from what had been his store window. He yelled excitedly, "What're you doing? Who broke my window?"

Harding managed a weak smile, but he was in pain. "Don't blame me. All I'm doing is lying here with a bullet hole in my side. The man who did the shooting is long gone. Is there a doctor anywhere close?"

Before the pawn shop owner could answer, a policeman came pounding down the street, his revolver in his hand. He took one look at Harding, holstered his gun, and asked, "How did it happen, mister?"

Harding struggled to his feet, assisted by the policeman. He looked down at the spreading red stain on his jacket.

"Someone was following me, a peg-legged man named Ike Langhorn. When I saw his reflection in the window and started to turn, he shot me. I didn't even get off a shot. If you don't believe me, look at my gun."

The policeman did, and sniffed the barrel. "You're right, it hasn't been fired lately. But I'm going to have to file a report just the same. What did you say his name was? Langfield?"

"Langhorn," Harding corrected. "But he's had time to get away by now. What I need is a doctor."

"How about my window?" the shop owner wailed.

"It'll cost ten dollars for a new one."

"Forget the window," the policeman said. "I've got to get this man to a doctor." He looked at Harding. "There's one in the next block. Do you think you can make it?"

"Sure," Harding said. "But first I'll pay for the window. If I hadn't seen Langhorn's reflection in it, I'd probably be dead." He took out a ten-dollar bill and handed it to the pawnbroker.

The doctor made Harding strip to the waist, and examined his side.

"You're very fortunate, my friend. The bullet glanced off a rib without breaking it. I wouldn't advise you to wrestle any bears for a few days, but with any kind of luck you'll be all right."

"Thanks," Harding said. "Now if you'll bandage me up, I'll pay you and be on my way."

At this, the policeman, who had left and come back, said mildly, "It won't be quite that simple, stranger. You'll have to come down to the station and answer some questions. I've already sent for the paddy wagon."

"Oh come on!" Harding groaned. "I'm not the villain in the play, just the innocent victim."

"That's for the captain to decide. We don't overlook shootings here in Denver the way we used to. I think I hear the paddy wagon now."

Harding paid the doctor, who had done a good job of bandaging him, and followed the policeman out of the office, favoring his left side. Disgusted with himself for having been outdrawn, and embarrassed at having to ride in a paddy wagon, he climbed in. The policeman followed, and sat beside him.

"Sorry about this, stranger. What's your name?"

"Harding. Allan Harding."

"Well, Mr. Harding, I don't think you're in much trouble. Like you said, you're the one who got shot, not the gunman. I've already put out an alarm for him. A one-legged man shouldn't be hard to find."

Unfortunately for the policeman's prediction, Langhorn had already hired a horse and was on his way back to Central City. He was under the impression that Harding was dead. It wasn't his habit to miss. Certainly not to miss the same man twice.

The other part of what the policeman had said was more accurate. After a brief questioning by the captain, Harding was allowed to leave. He hailed a hack, and went directly to the Ames Hotel, where he was able to rent a room on the third floor. Climbing the steps was an effort, but he would be high enough to so that nobody could reach his window.

Harding dozed fitfully the rest of the day, his side paining him considerably. Knowing that he couldn't afford to lose his strength, he left the hotel just before six o'clock and headed for the nearest restaurant. On the way he found a dry good store open and bought a shirt. His old one was torn and bloody. The blood didn't show much on his jacket, so he put it back on. He reached the restaurant and forced himself to eat a full meal, then went back to the hotel.

Morning found him still hurting, but he didn't feel feverish, so he hoped there was no infection. After settling his bill and eating breakfast, he went back to the wholesale house. Gibbs looked at him inquiringly.

"You're sort of peaked, Harding. What happened to you?"

"Some friendly gentleman shot me," Harding said. "But I'll be all right. Have you got my bill totaled?"

"Yes, sir." So he was now being called "sir." "It comes to two hundred five dollars and sixty-seven cents.

We'll forget the pennies."

"That's generous of you," Harding said, "But I like to pay in full." He counted out two hundred ten dollars and pocketed his change. "I suppose the shipment will go out on this morning's train?"

"It's already loaded. How do you intend to send future orders? You surely won't be making the trip in person?"

"No. One of us will mail it from Central City. We'll still be picking up other supplies there. And now I'd better hurry or I'll miss that train."

The ride back to Central City seemed even rougher, since every jolt made Harding's side hurt. He had been wondering how Langhorn had reached Denver as soon as he had, since he hadn't been one of the passengers. When the train stopped to take on water, Harding walked back to the caboose. The brakeman was standing on the rear platform, and Harding asked him, "Were you on the run from Central City yesterday?"

"I'm on every day," the man said. "Except Sundays, that is. Why?"

"Did you have a peg-legged man riding back here?"

"We sure did. Queer duck, if you ask me. He didn't open his mouth the whole trip. Friend of yours?"

"No," Harding said. "You might call him a business acquaintance. Thanks."

The train screeched to a stop in Central City, and Harding watched his order being unloaded onto a flat. Concerned that something might happen to it while he went for the wagon, he approached a man who was wearing a marshal's star.

"Can I ask a favor, Marshal?"

"Sure," the marshal said. From his attitude, he was in no big hurry to go any place. He had probably just come down to watch the train arrive.

"It's that flat of supplies," Harding said, pointing. "I have to go to the livery barn for a wagon, and I'm afraid something might happen to it. Can you keep an eye on it till I get back?"

"Sure thing," the marshal said. "Unless I get called away, which isn't likely."

"There's something else," Harding said. "I've got a bum side, and don't want to load the wagon myself. Do you suppose you could find someone to give me a hand?"

"I'll do it myself," the marshal said.

"I'll make it as fast as possible," Harding promised, and took off. He realized that Langhorn, on a horse, could have reached Central City ahead of him, so he kept a sharp lookout, but no trouble developed. When he got back with the wagon, and the marshal had helped him load it, Harding took out a five-dollar bill.

"I suppose you're not allowed to accept tips, but you can put this in the police widows and orphans fund."

"You bet," the marshal said. "Much obliged."

"By the way," Harding asked. "Have you noticed a one-legged man around here?"

"Not today, but there was one in town day before yesterday. You looking for him?"

"You might say so," Harding answered, and climbed up onto the wagon seat. It was late in the day to start for Leadville, but he decided to do it anyway. The sky was clear, and there would be a moon. More important, Durham's men wouldn't be expecting such a move. He jiggled the lines and pulled away from the depot.

Chapter Nineteen

Langhorn had ridden into Central City before dark, made arrangements for the return of his rented horse to Denver, and had gone back to the hotel in which he had spent the previous night. The following morning, while Harding was still asleep in Denver, Langhorn had reclaimed his own horse from the livery barn and headed for Leadville, confident that his trip to Denver had ended successfully.

Reaching Leadville in mid-afternoon, Langhorn rode directly to the Rocky Mountain Freight barn. Faraday, ostensibly in charge, was in the living quarters playing pinochle with Dobbs. Langhorn glanced around the barn and said acidly, "You sure did one hell of a job of filling in for me. This place looks like it hasn't been cleaned since I left."

Faraday, who was afraid of Langhorn, said defensively, "Moose didn't say anything about cleaning up; he just told me to keep an eye on things."

"You aren't even doing that. I could have walked off with a couple of horses and you wouldn't have known the difference. Get out there and get busy! Both of you."

"Now hold on," Dobbs protested, but changed his mind when he saw the look in Langhorn's eyes. He laid down his cards and followed Faraday out into the barn.

Langhorn went on foot to Durham's office, boldly approaching the front door, which he was surprised to find locked. When he knocked without results, he returned to the barn and confronted Faraday.

"Where's the boss?"

"He rode out to visit some of the mines. Seems Harding and the girl were out that way Monday, and Moose wants to find out what they were up to."

"You might have told me," Langhorn said. He put his saddle on a fresh horse, and rode out of the barn. Behind him, the two men exchanged glances.

"High and mighty bastard, ain't he?" Dobbs said. "What gives him the right to order us around?"

"'A little contraption made by a man named Colt," Faraday said sardonically. "Would you like to argue with it?"

"One of these days I just might," Dobbs muttered. "I ain't so slow with a sixgun myself."

"I'll come to your funeral," Faraday promised.

Moose Durham was trying to reason with the owner of Shamrock mine. "You're making a bad mistake, Casey. Harding's a fly-by-night. He won't last a month."

"He looks pretty substantial to me," Casey said. "And if he was what you say, Molly Root wouldn't be on his side."

"She's probably fallen for him," Durham said. "Women are like that about men with his looks."

"Not Molly," Casey said. "Or if she did, she wouldn't be fooled. She's got a level head on her shoulders."

"Well, just remember that I warned you. When Harding's outfit folds, you'll be begging me to haul your freight for you." He left the mine office and mounted his black stallion. He was still in an ugly mood when he met Langhorn on the road.

"Where the devil have you been? I expected you back yesterday."

"Harding went to Denver and I followed him. There

wasn't any way to let you know."

"Did you see what he did in Denver?"

"Yes, but it don't make any difference. He won't be coming back."

Durham looked at him sharply. "What does that mean?"

"Harding had an accident."

"Come out with it!" Durham snapped. "Did you kill him?"

Langhorn nodded, and Durham's lips tightened.

"I didn't tell you to do that. What if somebody saw you?"

"Do I look like a fool?" Langhorn demanded. "No one saw me except Harding, and he ain't about to talk. When the Denver cops find out he was from out of town, they'll lose interest. They might notify Dave Banks, and you know what that'll amount to."

They rode in silence for a mile or so while Durham considered the possible consequences. Finally he said, "I don't like your going against my orders, but what's done is done. Without Harding, their whole business will fold up. He was the brains behind it."

"Him and the Root girl," Langhorn said. "But she can't swing it alone. I don't see as you've got any kick coming. In fact you should pay me a bonus. Either that or give me a better job. I don't want to spend the rest of my life in that barn."

"I'll think about it," Durham promised. "With no competition, we'll be busier than ever. There might be something more interesting for you to do."

At the office of the Feeney Freight Lines, Frisco was talking with Molly.

"It looks like Harding was right about Langhorn being in Central City. Billy tells me he saw a peg-legged

145

man ride in from that direction an hour ago. I'm worried."

"You think of lot of your partner, don't you?"

"Danged right I do. We've been trailing along together for close to ten years. Did he ever tell you how we happened to meet?"

Molly shook her head.

"No," Frisco said. "I reckon he wouldn't. It was in a saloon. I'd got into an argument with some jasper . . . I wasn't as peaceable then as I am now . . . and found out too late that he had a sidekick behind me. They would've had me good and proper, but Harding, who didn't know me from Adam, grabbed the sidekick's gun hand before he could shoot me in the back."

"My goodness! What happened to the other man?"

"I don't rightly know," Frisco said. "It depends on the kind of life he'd led."

"You mean . . . doesn't it bother you at all?"

"Well, not as much as if it had turned out the other way," Frisco said. "But you didn't ask for my life history. Not changing the subject or anything, but I saw a fancy-looking woman coming out of the millinery. About your size, but with red hair. She looked familiar, somehow."

"That would be Lola Marchant, Durham's housekeeper."

"Well, Durham sure knows how to pick 'em," Frisco said, grinning. "Although she was a little flashy for my taste. Don't folks talk about a woman like her living in the same house with Durham and his sick wife?"

"Not out loud they don't," Molly said. "What are Gagan and Billy doing?"

"Gagan went to let Doc Mapes look him over. Billy's currying the horses. And both of them are worrying about Harding, the same as you and me."

146

Molly glanced out the window. "There's Durham now, and Ike Langhorn with him."

Frisco moved up beside her. "So that's Langhorn, is it? He's a tough-looking hombre."

"From what I hear, he's as tough as he looks," Molly said. "I wonder why he decided to show himself. He's been keeping out of sight since you and Allan reached town."

Frisco noticed the "Allan," but didn't comment. Instead, he said, "It looks as if he figures that it don't matter any more. Whether we see him or not, that is. Now I really am worried. He shoots at Harding from ambush, and then stays out of sight, but now he's bold as you please."

"We're not sure it was him," Molly said.

"Maybe you ain't, but I am. Else why did he follow us to Central City?"

"You're not sure of that, either. You didn't actually see him there."

"I ain't seen the Pacific Ocean," Frisco said. "Nor the other one, either, but I believe they're there. I'd like to ask Langhorn point blank if he's seen my partner."

"Don't do it," Molly begged. "He'd just deny it if he has, and if you made an issue of it, you'd probably end up in Dave Banks's jail. Either there or the graveyard."

"Yeah. Well, I'll give Harding another twenty-four hours. If he hasn't shown up by then, I'm going after Langhorn, come hell or high water."

It was still night when Harding reached Leadville. He drove to the Feeney barn, unlocked the door, and was swinging it open when a voice said, "Don't move or I'll shoot!"

"Billy!" Harding said quickly. "I'd clean forgotten you were sleeping in the barn."

"Mr. Harding? What in the dickens . . ."

147

"I thought it would be safer traveling at night," Harding explained. "Drive the wagon in, will you? I'm about played out."

"Sure thing," Billy said. He drove the wagon inside, and closed the doors. "Are you all right?"

"Well, I've got a bullet hole over my ribs, but I'll be okay once I get a few hours' sleep."

"Use my blankets. I won't be going back to bed anyway. Who shot you?"

"I'll tell you about it later. Meanwhile, though, a couple of instructions. I don't think anybody but you saw me come in. When you go to Hetty Cook's for breakfast, keep still about my being here. I'll tell you why when I'm not so sleepy."

"I'll be careful," Billy promised. "And I'm glad you're back. We've all been worried about you."

"Thanks. Good night. Or should I say good morning?"

Chapter Twenty

Seated at the breakfast table, Frisco looked at Billy speculatively. "What's itchin' you, boy? You look like you just stepped on a rattlesnake."

"Me?" Billy said, trying to sound casual. "Nothing's itchin' me. I just didn't sleep very well last night."

"Neither did I," Molly Root said. "I was worrying about Allan Harding. I hope nothing's happened to him."

Billy was hard put not to blurt out the truth, that Harding was back and in the Feeney barn. Since Guillford was present, he restrained himself. Once he and Molly and Frisco were on their way to the barn, though, and no one else was within hearing distance, he could contain himself no longer.

"Mr. Harding is all right. He got back from Central City during the night."

"Well I'll be!" Frisco snorted. "You sure took your time letting us know."

"He told me not to say anything to anybody, but I don't think that included you two, since you'll know it anyway in a few minutes."

"He must have something up his sleeve," Frisco said. "Anyway, I'm glad he's back."

"So am I," Molly said, smiling with relief. "After the bold way Ike Langhorn showed himself yesterday, I imagined all sorts of things." She began to hurry, but Frisco took her by the arm.

"Better not act any different than usual. Someone

might be watching, and get curious. And don't look so happy."

Molly erased the smile from her face, and they proceded at a more leisurely pace. Once they reached the barn, however, and Frisco had opened the door, she hurried inside. Harding, standing well away from the doorway, grinned and said, "Don't look so startled. It's only me."

"Thank goodness you're back!" Molly said. "Why didn't you come up to the house for breakfast?"

"Just a wild idea of mine," Harding said, and looked past her at Frisco.

"Did you worry about me, partner?"

"Shucks no," Frisco said. "I never gave it a thought. But what's this wild idea of yours?"

"Well, I didn't tell Billy, but Ike Langhorn followed me to Denver and shot me."

"Shot you!" Molly gasped.

"It was just a scratch," Harding assured her. "But it knocked me down, and I think Langhorn believes I'm dead. Which I probably would be, if I hadn't seen his reflection in time to duck. I suppose Durham thinks so, too. I intend to keep out of sight for a while and see what happens."

"So that's why Langhorn quit hiding out," Molly said. "He showed himself yesterday for the first time since you reached town. Say, you must be hungry."

"Starved," Harding agreed. "Here I am with a whole wagon load of provisions, and nothing suitable to eat without cooking."

"Let me go back to Hetty Cook's and get you something," Molly offered, but Harding shook his head.

"It will be better for you to act like nothing's happened. Go into the office and start a fire. Folks expect to see smoke coming out of the stovepipe. I've missed meals before.''

Spud Gagan came in just then, and said, ''Morning, everybody. I see we've got a full crew again.'' He pointed at Harding's torn jacket. ''What happened?''

''Ike Langhorn creased me with a bullet. I'm guessing that he thinks I'm done for, so don't let on that you know different.''

''Whatever you say,'' Gagan agreed. ''I see you also brought back the load of supplies. Do you want them put on the shelves?''

''That's right. We won't start using any of them until we've built up a bigger stock. The next time someone goes to Central City for a load, we'll mail another order to Denver.''

''That'll be today,'' Frisco said. ''Molly says there'll be an order to pick up tomorrow.''

''Good. Billy, you and Gagan can make the run. I don't think anybody will bother you. Not if Durham thinks I'm out of the picture. You can take the empty wagon. Frisco and I will unload the one I just brought in.''

Molly came out of the office. ''The fire's going. Do you know we have a load to pick up in Central City?''

''Frisco was just telling me. I wish you'd write up another order for the wholesaler in Denver. Billy and Gagan can mail it from Central City, and we'll pick it up later. About the same size as this last one.''

Molly nodded and went back into the office. A moment later she poked her head through the doorway and said, ''Moose Durham just entered his office.''

Gagan and Billy took Billy's bedding out of the empty wagon and began preparing it for the trip to Central City. Frisco, refusing Harding's help, started transferring the newly arrived merchandise to the shelves.

''You better not strain yourself, boy. I've got an idea

151

your side don't feel so good.''

"It has felt better," Harding admitted. "But I'll be all right. Some doctor in Denver patched me up. Man, I could sure use one of Hetty Cook's breakfasts!"

By nine o'clock Billy and Gagan had driven off, Frisco had finished stocking the shelves, and Molly was busy in the office. Across the street, Moose Durham came to a decision. He put on his hat, left the office, and crossed toward the Feeney barn. Harding, who was watching from back in the shadows, saw him coming and ducked out of sight.

Molly looked up in surprise as there was a knock on the office door and a voice she recognized as Durham's called, "Can I come in?"

"It's unlocked," Molly called back, wondering what in the world Durham could want. He had never set foot inside the Feeney building during the time she had been working there.

Durham, who could be very gracious when it suited his purposes, came into the office. "Sorry to bother you, Miss Root, but I'd like to speak to Mr. Harding."

"He isn't here," Molly said, stretching the truth a little, since she assumed that Allan was still in the back part of the barn.

"Any idea when he will be?"

Molly shook her head. If Allan wanted Durham to think he was dead, she wasn't going to spoil the illusion.

"He went to Central City. Is there anything I can do for you?"

"You can give him a message," Durham said. "I've been thinking about this rate war. We're both going to lose money, and there's no point in it. Leadville doesn't need two freighting outfits anyway. I've decided to buy him out."

"Isn't this rather sudden?" Molly asked. "I mean

you never offered to buy out Mr. Feeney."

"Just deliver the message," Durham said, and added as an afterthought, "if you please."

"Why don't you deliver it yourself?" Harding asked, stepping through the doorway.

Durham whirled, and for a moment he couldn't conceal his surprise.

"I thought—" He broke off in a mid-sentence, so Harding finished it for him.

"That I was dead. Is that what you were going to say?" He shook hs head. "I'm afraid you overestimate your man Langhorn. He's not infallible after all. In fact he's missed me twice."

"I don't know what you're talking about," Durham said, regaining his composure. "If you overheard what I just told this girl, you know why I came here. My offer still stands. I'm willing to buy you out for your nuisance value."

Harding smiled. "You probably don't know how much of a nuisance I can be. But that wasn't your real reason for coming. You wanted to make sure I hadn't returned from Central City. However, I'm willing to overlook that little fib. If you really want to buy us out, make an offer. Anything over fifty thousand."

"You're crazy!"

"Maybe so," Harding acknowledged. "But not crazy enough to do business with a man who hires his killing done. Besides, I have a certain amount of sympathy for the mine owners. If you had the only freighting outfit in town, you'd rob them blind."

Durham didn't answer, but stalked toward the doorway, his face contorted with anger. Harding stepped aside to let him pass, then followed him out into the barn and through the big doorway. As they reached the street, movement on the other side made Harding look up. Ike Langhorn was just outside Durham's office, reaching for the door. He stared at Harding in stunned disbelief, then, without a word of warning, made a grab for his gun

This time Harding was ready for him. His own pistol came into his hand, and he squeezed the trigger. The two shots were almost simultaneous. Almost, but not quite. Langhorn was knocked down as a bullet slammed into his chest. His own slug missed Harding by inches.

Harding swung his gun toward Durham, but Durham stood as though turned to stone. If he was carrying a concealed weapon, he had sense enough not to try for it.

Molly and Frisco came running out of the barn, Frisco with his gun fisted. Several people on the sidewalk turned to stare, and a buggy drew to a stop in front of the livery stable. Marshal Banks came running from the direction of his office. He skidded to a stop, and demanded loudly, "What's going on here?"

Harding seemed to recall having heard the marshal ask that same question before. He holstered his gun and turned to look squarely at the lawman.

"Ike Langhorn tried to gun me down. I outdrew him."

Marshal Banks looked at Durham. "Is that the way it was, Mr. Durham?"

Durham seemed about to reply, then glanced up to see that the buggy had pulled up in front of the Feeney barn. The driver was Dr. Mapes, who was watching the scene intently. After a brief hesitation, Durham said, "It happened so fast I can't say who started it."

"I can," Dr. Mapes said from the buggy. "And it wasn't Mr. Harding. Langhorn went for his gun first, but he wasn't fast enough." He got down from the buggy and crossed over to look at the fallen man, then said bluntly, "He's dead."

154

Marshal Banks seemed to be over his depth. He cleared his throat and asked uneasily, "Why would Langhorn try to kill you, Harding?"

"Probably for the same reason he tried it in Denver," Harding said. "And ambushed Guillford and me last Saturday night here on the street. Maybe Durham can answer your question."

Durham shook his head. "I know nothing about it." He looked at Harding. "I hope you're not accusing me of having anything to do with it."

"Me accuse you?" Harding said. "In Leadville? I'm not that foolish. Not when you've got the law in your pocket."

"Now just a minute!" Banks protested, but he didn't seem at all sure of himself. "You've got no business saying that. And what's this about Denver?"

"Check with the Denver police," Harding said. "You'll probably be hearing from them anyway. In the meantime, if you have any complaints, let's hear them here in front of witnesses."

The marshal tugged nervously at his ear, and shook his head. "If Doc says you didn't draw first, that's good enough for me." He looked at Durham and added, "Unless you've got something to say, Mr. Durham."

Durham didn't answer, but walked across toward his office. He had to step over Langhorn's body to reach the door. The marshal, looking relieved, motioned toward a couple of men among the group which had gathered.

"Give me a hand. We've got to get Langhorn to the undertaker's."

Harding turned and went back into the barn. Molly would have followed him, but Frisco held her back.

"Suppose we leave him alone for a while. Now that

it's over, he probably feels shaky."

Molly nodded understandingly and went into the office. She, too, was beginning to tremble. Frisco, who had been in similar situations before, stood silently in the doorway and watched them pick up the earthly remains of Ike Langhorn.

Chapter Twenty-One

As Frisco had guessed, Harding was undergoing the reaction from having killed another human being. He had experienced this before, and knew that it would pass. When it did, he went in and told Molly where he was going, then walked to the boarding house, where Hetty Cook gave him a late breakfast, despite the fact that it was Friday, her day for the weekly house cleaning. Knowing that he would be underfoot, Harding left immediately after eating, and returned to the main street. Instead of going back to the barn, he went through the saddle shop to the newspaper office.

Stacy Guillford, folding freshly printed copies of the *Courier* looked up at him and said eagerly, "You're just in time to tell me what you think of my editorial."

Harding accepted the paper Guillford handed him, and moved over to the better light by a window. On the front page, under the heading FREEDOM OF THE PRESS, was the article. Harding read it, and turned to look at Guillford.

"If you want my personal opinion, it's excellent. Of course you realize that it will make Moose Durham spit nails."

"I didn't mention his name."

"No, but you might as well have. Everybody who reads it will know it's him you're talking about. For a peaceful-looking man you've put yourself in a dangerous position. Doesn't it worry you?"

"Of course it does," Guillford said. "I'm the worrying type. But it was something I felt I had to say.

If I wanted to be melodramatic, I'd say it was a matter of principle. Fearless editor and all that nonsense. Speaking of danger, I understand you had a narrow escape this morning. Tell me about it.''

"There's not a great deal to tell. Ike Langhorn tried to shoot me, and I was lucky.''

"That much I knew, although I'm not sure it was luck. But there must be more to it than that. Remember, you're talking to a newspaperman. I have the when, the where, and the who, but not the why.''

Harding considered this a moment and shrugged. "Marshal Banks already knows, so it's no secret. Langhorn took a shot at me in Denver. Presumably he thought he killed me, so when he saw me this morning, he went a little haywire. Actually, I wouldn't have started it. I don't hanker to end up in jail. Which is where I'd probably be right now if Doc Maples hadn't seen the whole thing.''

"And you said there wasn't a great deal to tell,'' Guillford said drily. "Wait till you read next week's *Courier*.''

"Well, for Pete's sake don't write an editorial about it.''

"I won't,'' Guillford promised. "By the way, you haven't said anything about your ad. Is it all right?''

Harding had been too interested in the editorial to look any farther. He did so now, and found the full-page advertisement for Feeney Freight Lines.

"It's fine. A lot better than if I'd written it myself. I suppose we ought to drop the name Feeney, but there's no hurry.'' He took out his wallet and handed over fifty dollars. "Next week I'll have a different advertisement. We're going to set up a local warehouse and keep it stocked. I'll give you the details later.'' He grinned, and added, "Provided you and I are still around. I'm sure

158

Durham would like to see us both in our graves. You might be wise to start carrying a gun.''

"The pen is mightier than the sword," Guillford said. "Especially since I wouldn't know how to use a gun if I had one. Someday nobody will have to go around armed.''

"Don't hold your breath," Harding said, and left the shop.

Walking back to the barn, he was conscious of being the center of attention. By now everyone would know that he had killed Ike Langhorn. It was a distinction he wouldn't have chosen.

Moose Durham, scowling behind his desk, saw Harding return to the Feeney barn, and mouthed an obscenity. Lucky bastard. If Doc Mapes hadn't happened along at the wrong time, Harding would be in jail. Instead, Harding was free, and Ike Langhorn was dead. Not that the fool didn't deserve it, starting a gunfight on the main street in broad daylight. Still, he had been a cog in Durham's organization. A cog which would have to be replaced. Maybe Faraday . . .

Too angry to concentrate, Durham left the office and went home. It was an hour before noon, not yet time for dinner, and his wife Clara, sitting listlessly in a rocking chair in the parlor, looked up at him in mild surprise.

"Is something wrong?"

"Everything's wrong, dammit!" Durham growled. "Oh what's the use? You wouldn't know what I was talking about." He stormed into his study and came to an abrupt halt as he saw Lola Marchant seated at his desk.

"What the devil are you doing here?"

"Reading the *Courier*," Lola said casually. "It was just now delivered. There's an editorial that should interest you."

"Dammit!" Durham exploded. "You've got your gall, sitting at my desk and reading my paper. I've told you to leave this room alone. You aren't paid to sit around and read."

"We both know what I'm paid for," Lola said, with a shrug. She got up and moved past him to close the door into the hall. "And since you've brought up the subject, I'm getting tired of waiting. When are you going to get rid of your wife?"

Durham looked at her narrowly. "What's that supposed to mean?"

"Whatever you want it to," Lola said. "You don't necessarily have to kill her. Just send her away someplace. Maybe to a sanitarium in Denver. I'm fed up with pussyfooting around like some sort of servant."

"I'll decide what has to be done," Durham said harshly. "Any time you're dissatisfied, you can leave."

Lola's eyes flashed. "Oh no you don't! You promised."

"To hell with what I promised! I've got enough troubles without listening to your whining. Give me that paper and get out of here."

"You cheap son of a bitch!"

Already near the boiling point, Durham brought the back of his hand across her cheek, knocking her down. She rose slowly to her feet, and said ominously, "You're going to be sorry for that. No man hits Lola Marchant and gets away with it." Holding a hand to her cheek, she left the study.

Durham was appalled at what he had done. He prided himself on having self-control. Something was getting into him lately.

After a bit he shrugged it off and picked up the paper she had dropped. By the time he finished reading the editorial, he had completely forgotten the incident. For a long while he sat at his desk, considering what to do about Stacy Guillford.

Harding, after a good night's sleep, was back almost to normal. Frisco, watching him shave, asked curiously, "What do you suppose Durham will do, now that you've killed his top gun? Come after you himself?"

"I doubt it," Harding said. "He still has Dobbs and Faraday, not to mention others that we may not know about. But I think he'll bide his time. To tell the truth, right now I'm more worried about Stacy Guillford. That was a pretty outspoken editorial he published. Durham must be furious."

"Yeah," Frisco agreed. "Guillford's got guts. But that's his problem, not ours. Let's eat."

There were only four at breakfast, since Billy was at Central City with Gagan. Afterward, Harding walked with Molly and Frisco to the barn, assured himself that everything there was in order, and left, telling them he would be back shortly. His concern about Guillford was stronger than ever, and he wanted to talk with him.

The Mexican saddlemaker looked distressed, and Harding hurried into the print shop. He found Guillford standing in the midst of a rubble of scattered type, broken furniture, and torn paper.

Guillford turned to look at him and tried to grin. "You warned me, Harding, but I didn't anticipate anything like this."

"Durham doesn't waste time," Harding commented. "Will this put you out of business?"

"Not permanently. They didn't know enough to wreck the printing press. But it'll take a week to get back into production. Oh Lord, when I think of sorting out that type!"

"Have you reported this to the marshal?"

"No. Do you think it would do any good? I mean in view of what we both think of him."

"He probably won't do much about it, but I believe you ought to tell him. He'll at least have to put up a bluff. If you want to talk to him, I'd like to go along."

"All right," Guillford said. "He might at least take a look at the wreckage before I start cleaning it up."

Marshal Banks was in his office in front of the jail. He looked up warily.

"Well? What's on your minds?"

Guillford said, "I want to report a crime. During the night, somebody vandalized my shop. I'd like you to see what they did."

Banks debated with himself a moment, then rose heavily to his feet.

"Chances are it was a bunch of kids. They'll do almost anything nowadays."

"It wasn't kids," Harding said. "Did you read Guillford's editorial in this week's *Courier*?"

"I haven't time to read newspapers," Banks said.

"Maybe you should *make* time," Harding suggested. "Occasionally they're more enlightening than that dime western on your desk."

Banks didn't try to answer this, but he couldn't help looking embarrassed. Without another word, he followed them out the door. After a cursory inspection of the newspaper shop, he said carelessly, "Like I said, it was probably kids. I'll see what I can turn up."

"Like I said, it wasn't kids," Harding told him. "There's such a thing as coincidence, but this is stretching it too far. Guillford printed an editorial aimed at Moose Durham, and that same night his shop was wrecked."

"Are you claiming that Durham did it?"

"Not in person," Harding said. "My first choice would be Dobbs and Faraday. I think you ought to ask them a few questions. If you don't, I will."

"Now, listen here! You aren't going to take the law into your own hands. Not in my town."

"If it's your town, you'd better protect it," Harding said. "I'll come along. You can deputize me if you want to."

"Like hell I will!"

"Then I'll just be an interested observer. Where would you expect to find that pair at this time of day?"

"Who knows?" the marshal said. "They might be out on the road somewhere for all I know."

"I doubt it," Harding said. He turned to Guillford. "Do you know where they live?"

Before Guillford could answer, the marshal said irritably, "I know the place, dammit. All right, I'll go talk to them, but I don't need your help."

"I think I'll trail along anyway," Harding said. "Mr. Guillford, you might as well come along, too. This could be a story for your newspaper."

Muttering to himself, Banks stomped through the saddle shop, flanked by Harding and Guillford. The place to which he led them was a rickety shack on the edge of town. He banged his knuckles on the door, and nothing happened.

"Like I said, they're probably out somewhere."

"Try again," Harding said. "I saw a curtain move."

Tight-lipped, the marshal pounded on the door. "This is Dave Banks. Open up. I know you're there."

Silence for a moment, then there were soft footsteps, and the door was opened a few inches. Faraday said innocently, "You woke us up, Marshal. What do you want?"

"To talk to you, dammit. Let me in."

Faraday opened the door wider, and the marshal entered. Harding motioned for Guillford to stay outside, and followed the marshal. Faraday, who had ostensibly been asleep, was wearing only long johns. Dobbs was still in his bunk, looking more worried than sleepy. Faraday said, "Now that you've woke us up, let's hear what you have to say."

The marshal cleared his throat self-consciously. "Have you two been here all night?"

"Of course we have," Faraday said. "We came home right after the Ace of Spades closed. Why?"

Harding noted that Dobbs was keeping his hands out of sight under the blanket. The man's holstered gun was hanging on a nail beside the bunk. Keeping his eyes on Dobbs, Harding said, "Take a look at Faraday's hands, Marshal. I think you'll find printer's ink."

Faraday frowned at the marshal. "Have you got a warrant or something? A man's home is supposed to be his castle."

"Now don't go throwing the law at me," Banks said. "You opened the door and let me in. How come you're so touchy about letting me see your hands?"

Over on the bunk, the blanket moved. Harding let his hand rest on his gun, and the movement stopped.

Faraday shrugged, and turned up his palms. They were stained with ink.

"All right, Marshal, so we messed up the print shop a little. What's so terrible about that? We was just having some fun."

Still watching Dobbs, Harding said, "Ask him who put them up to it, Marshal."

"Nobody," Faraday said, without giving Banks time to ask the question. "It was our own idea. Maybe we'd had a little too much to drink."

"Well, I'm going to have to arrest you," Banks said.

"Put on your clothes, both of you."

Harding backed out of the room, Guillford stepping aside to let him pass. As they headed toward the main street, Guillford said, "That was quick. I'll feel safer with those two in jail."

"Better not feel too safe," Harding warned. "I've got an idea they'll be out soon. Courtesy of Moose Durham."

Chapter Twenty-Two

It didn't take long for word of the arrest to reach the Ace of Spades, where one of the Rocky Mountain drivers picked it up and relayed it to Durham. Durham feigned surprise, since he was not supposed to know about the wrecking of Guillford's shop. His anger, however, was genuine, and he made no effort to conceal it. Banks must be crazy, arresting Durham's men. Durham slammed out of his office and walked rapidly to the jail, where he found Dave Banks at his desk, and Dobbs and Faraday in a cell.

Durham barely glanced at the prisoners before fixing his angry gaze on the marshal.

"What the devil's the meaning of this? You should know better than to throw my men in jail. I want them out of here damned fast."

The marshal looked as uncomfortable as he felt. He said apologetically, "I couldn't very well help it, Mr. Durham. They, or at least Faraday, admitted busting up the *Courier* office, and both of them had ink on their hands.

"You had no business going after them in the first place," Durham said.

"I couldn't help that, either," Banks protested. "Harding said—"

"Damn Harding! He's a troublemaker. Since when have you been taking orders from him?"

Banks licked his lips nervously. "It wasn't orders, exactly. He said if I wouldn't go, he'd go himself. Then he insisted on tagging along with me. Him and Guillford both. There wasn't any way I could stop them. Harding followed me right into the house, and he's the one who wanted to see Faraday's hands."

"You could have avoided it somehow," Durham said. "Harding's got you buffaloed." He walked back to the cells, and faced Faraday through the bars. In a voice loud enough for the marshal to hear, he asked, "What gave you the idea of breaking into Guillford's shop?"

Faraday, knowing what was expected of him, said with a shrug, "It's like I told the marshal. We'd had a few too many drinks, and it seemed like a good joke. It don't seem so funny now."

"Well, I should hope not," Durham said, and returned to the front of the office.

"I want these men out of here. How much bail will it take?"

Banks, thoroughly miserable, said reluctantly, "It ain't going to be quite that easy, Mr. Durham. In a case like this, it's up to the judge to set bail."

"You know damned well the judge is out of town."

"Yes, sir, but he's due back on the next stage. I'll talk to him as soon as he comes in. They ought to be out in practically no time."

"They'd better be!" Durham said, and stormed out of the building. He returned to his office, where he sat staring at his desk. Langhorn was dead, and now two of his men were in jail. That didn't leave anybody for the kind of job he had in mind. He'd have to handle it himself. He left the office and went to the livery stable. Minutes later he rode out on his black stallion and headed toward the mines.

So far as the Feeney Freight Lines were concerned, the rest of the day was uneventful, in fact Harding, using the empty wagon as a bed, took time to catch up on some of the sleep he had missed the night before. Just before supper time Spud Gagan and Billy Gregg pulled in with their load of supplies. Since this was an order for one of the mines, it wasn't necessary to unload it.

"Have any trouble?" Harding asked.

Gagan shook his head. "Everything went smooth as silk. That feller in Central City treated us real nice. I think he's beginning to be afraid of losing our business."

"Did you mail the order to Denver?"

"Sure did," Gagan told him. "I took it to the depot myself."

"Good," Harding said, and turned to Billy. "How do you like being a freighter by now?"

"Just fine," Billy said. "But it ain't as exciting as I expected it to be."

Harding grinned. "You'll get your fill of excitement before long. I killed Ike Langhorn yesterday morning, and Dobbs and Faraday are in jail for smashing up Guillford's shop. Durham isn't likely to sit still for it."

"Good gosh!" Billy exclaimed. "How did you come to kill Langhorn?"

Harding told him about it, with Gagan an interested listener. He finished by saying, "I don't know what Durham will do, but just to be safe, I'm going to spend the night with you here in the barn. We can take turns standing guard."

Frisco, who had been unharnessing the horses, spoke up. "How about you and me doing it, partner? We're the ones Durham's mad at. Billy's just an innocent bystander."

"That's right," Harding acknowledged, and turned to face Billy.

168

"What do you say, boy? You can use our bed in the boarding house if you want to."

"I'd rather stay here," Billy said.

"Then that settles it. Let's all go get supper."

Supper over, Billy returned to the barn alone, letting himself in through the front door. Harding took a devious route to reach the back of the building, where Billy admitted him through the rear door. Keeping his voice low, Harding said, "If there's trouble, it'll probably take place after midnight, when the Saturday night crowd has gone home. You take the first watch, and wake me up at twelve o'clock."

"What kind of trouble do you expect?" Billy asked.

"I'm not sure. Probably none. With Langhorn dead, and Dobbs and Faraday in jail, Durham's short-handed. I'm just being careful. Be sure to wake me up at midnight. Or sooner, if you see or hear anything suspicious."

"Yes, sir," Billy said. He picked up his rifle and went into the dark office, where he could watch the street through the window.

It wasn't yet midnight when Harding was awakened by Billy shaking his shoulder. Instantly alert, Harding asked softly, "What's wrong?"

"I heard someone moving around out back," Billy whispered. "It may have nothing to do with us, but I thought you'd want to know."

"You thought right," Harding said. He slid out of the wagon in which he had been sleeping, eased the gun out of his holster, and let himself out through the front door. He was halfway down the side of the building when there was a loud explosion at the far corner. Harding raced to the back of the building and was in time to see a man running away. He got off one quick shot, and the man broke stride for a second, then continued running.

There wasn't time to follow him now. Harding returned to the front of the building, flung open the big door, and rushed inside, calling, "Billy? Are you all right?"

If there was an answer, it was drowned out by the horses thrashing around in their stalls. Flames were already licking at the back wall of the barn. The horses would have to be driven outside, but first there was Billy to think of. Harding found him lying on his back near the spot where the explosion had taken place. Without checking to determine whether he was dead or alive, he picked him up and carried him out into the street.

A number of late hangers-on from the saloon had been attracted by the explosion. Harding motioned to them and said, "There's horses in the barn. Get them out!"

Whether it was the tone of his voice, or the fact that no one wanted a horse to burn, several of the men ran into the barn and began leading out the horses. By now the building was well ablaze, but Harding paid it no attention. He had determined that Billy was still alive, so he picked him up and headed for Doc Mape's place.

Luckily, the doctor was not out on a call. He answered Harding's shout, and opened the door, motioning Harding inside.

"Lay him over there. Has he been shot?"

"No," Harding said, placing Billy on the table. "There was an explosion at the barn, and it did something to him. He's been out ever since it happened."

Dr. Mapes was already making an examination. He straightened up and said with relief, "There don't appear to be any broken bones or wounds. He's got a bad bump on his head. Probably the explosion knocked him down and he banged into something."

"Then he'll be all right?"

"I didn't say that. He might have a fractured skull. I won't know until he comes to."

"Is there anything I can do?"

"Not a thing," Dr. Mapes told him. "You've likely got other things on your mind. Do you know who set off the blast?"

"I'm ninety percent sure," Harding said. "But that will have to wait. Right now I'm going back and see if it's possible to save the barn."

In the short time Harding had been gone, a dozen men had formed a bucket brigade, but it was only too obvious that their efforts would be of no avail. The whole barn was now ablaze. Frisco and Molly Root were there, along with most of the townspeople. Frisco reached Harding's side and asked anxiously, "Did Billy get out?"

"He's over at Dr Mapes's," Harding said. "Doc won't know how bad off he is until he comes to."

"Did you see who did it?"

"I got a glimpse of him," Harding said. "And I think I winged him, but I couldn't follow to make sure."

"Durham?"

"That's my guess," Harding said. "Damn a man who'd blow up a barn with horses in it!" He turned to Molly. "I didn't have time to save anything in the office. Will it make a lot of difference?"

Molly shook her head. "Nothing will make much difference now, with both wagons burned, and our stock of merchandise ruined. Not to mention the building." She managed a wry smile. "I guess Mr. Feeney was smart to get out when he did. It's too bad you and Frisco have to be the ones to suffer."

"Don't count us out yet," Harding said. "Excuse me, there's Marshal Banks. I want to talk to him."

Banks was standing with the rest of the spectators, making no effort to help. Not that there was much he could do. The bucket brigade had already given up on saving the barn, and were merely putting out sparks which might set another building afire. Banks saw Harding coming and moved out from the crowd.

"How did it happen, Harding? Did someone turn over a lamp?"

"It didn't just happen," Harding said. "The fire was deliberately set. Didn't you hear the explosion?"

"No. I was at the other end of town."

"You seem to have a talent for being as far from trouble as possible," Harding said. "How about Dobbs and Faraday? Are they still in jail?"

"They sure are," Banks said. "Mr. Durham wanted to bail them out, but I told him he'd have to wait for the judge."

"That narrows it down some," Harding said. "With Langhorn dead, and those two hardcases in jail, Durham might not have had anybody to do his dirty work. Except himself, that is."

"Now wait a minute! Are you accusing Durham of setting off the explosion?"

"Let's just say I'd like to know where he was half an hour ago. I suggest that we go to his house and find out."

By now the group had lost interest in the fire, and were listening to Harding and the marshal. Banks, apparently aware of them, looked decidedly uncomfortable. Harding took advantage of this by saying clearly, "Of course if you're afraid of Durham, I can go myself. Some of these folks around here will probably follow along out of curiosity."

"I'll go," Banks said. "But I'm warning you right now that you're making a bad mistake. You've got no reason to suspect Mr. Durham."

"I'll know more about that when I find out if he has a fresh bullet wound," Harding said. "Let's go."

172

Chapter Twenty-Three

Durham's leg, which Harding's bullet had hit, was bleeding badly by the time he reached his house. The place was dark, but almost at once Lola Marchant came into the front hall, carrying a lamp. She looked at him coldly, and said without concern, "You're spilling blood on the floor. What happened?"

"Never mind the questions," Durham retorted. "Just get a clean cloth I can wrap around my leg. And make it snappy!"

Lola left the hall, to come back presently with something suitable for a bandage. Durham pulled up his pants leg to expose a shallow gash in his calf. Lola knelt down and bandaged it. She straightened up and said curiously, "I heard a loud noise a few minutes ago. What was it?"

"I don't know," Durham lied. "I was taking a short-cut home, and some drunken miner shot me. Get some water and mop up the blood before it soaks into the floor."

"Don't you ever say please?"

"All right, dammit, please get some water. I'm going to bed, and you do the same. And remember, if anybody comes asking questions, I've been here all evening. Understand?"

Lola didn't answer, but went to the kitchen for some water and a mop. She didn't believe a word Durham had told her, but it was none of her business. She mopped up the blood as best she could, returned mop and bucket to the kitchen, and went to bed. Before she could go back to sleep, there was a knock at the front door. She got up, put on a robe over her nightgown, and went to answer it.

Durham was ahead of her, wearing a night shirt which he had tucked into a pair of pants, not the ones with the bullet hole. His hair was tousled as though he had been asleep.

"Well, Marshal, what is it this time? It better be important, waking me up at this hour of the night."

"Just a couple of questions," Banks said. "We can talk better inside."

Durham moved over to let him enter, and Harding, who had been standing in the shadows, followed him in.

"What's *he* doing here?" Durham demanded, and to Harding, "Get out. You can't come in."

"Oh, I think I can," Harding said mildly. "There's a bunch of men outside who will think it's strange if you don't let me in."

Durham hesitated a moment, then said grudgingly, "All right, but don't get the idea you're welcome." He turned to face Banks. "As long as you're here, let's have the questions."

Banks glanced at Lola, who had come into the hall, then returned his attention to Durham.

"Do you know that the Feeney barn has been burned to the ground?"

"The devil you say! This is the first I've heard of it. How did the fire start?"

"Someone set off a charge of dynamite. Didn't you hear the explosion?"

"I was asleep. I didn't feel so good tonight, so I turned in early." He gestured toward Lola. "She can back me up on that."

Banks looked at Lola. "Is that true, Miss

174

Marchant?''

Lola touched her cheek, which was still slightly pink where Durham had slapped her. She looked at Durham with what might have been satisfaction.

"Actually, Marshal, I can't say one way or the other. You see I was asleep, too. I didn't wake up until I heard the explosion."

Harding was watching Durham. If looks could kill, Lola would have dropped dead.

There was another knock at the door, and Durham called, "Who's there?"

"It's me, Doctor Mapes. Open up."

Unwillingly, Durham opened the door long enough for Doc Mapes to enter. "What are you *doing* here?"

"From what I heard in front of the Feeney barn, I figured there might be trouble. I came along to stop it if I could, or patch up the survivors if I couldn't." Doc glanced around. "Where's Mrs. Durham?"

"She's in her bedroom," Durham said. "She's a sound sleeper." He turned back to the marshal.

"You said you had a couple of questions. What's the other one?"

Banks would have given a month's pay to be somewhere else. Since this was impossible, he said nervously, "Harding took a shot at the man who was running away, and thinks he hit him."

"Harding again!" Durham growled. "By God, Marshal, I'm beginning to think he's running the town. He killed my top man, had two others thrown in jail, and now he's here to . . ." He turned his eyes on Harding. "Just what *are* you here for, Harding? Are you accusing me of starting the fire?"

"I'm not accusing you of anything," Harding said. "Not yet, anyway. I'd just like to find out if you've got a fresh bullet wound. That ought to be easy to settle, now that Doc's here to make the examination.''

"No one's going to make an examination," Durham declared. "In fact you're all going to leave. Pronto!"

"Not me," Harding said evenly. "Not unless I'm convinced you're not the man I shot. If you won't let Doc examine you, I'll pull off your clothes myself." He took a step towards Durham, but came to an abrupt halt as Lola said sharply, "Don't try it, mister! This gun is loaded."

Harding swung his eyes in Lola's direction and saw that she was holding a small revolver in her hand. At this distance, it could be as deadly as a .45. He supposed she must have had it in the pocket of her robe.

Rather surprisingly, since she had apparently come to Durham's defense, the look he gave her was hostile. Before he could say anything, however, his wife appeared in the inner doorway. She had to hold onto the door for support, but it seemed to Harding that she looked more alert than he would have expected. She asked mildly, "What's all the commotion about?"

Durham swivelled his gaze to his wife. "Nothing that concerns you. Why aren't you asleep?"

Mrs. Durham's lips twitched, almost as though she were amused. She said mildly, "I didn't drink my tea tonight. She . . ." She pointed at Lola. "She thinks I did, but when she wasn't looking, I poured it in the chamber pot."

Doc Mapes spoke up.

"What are you talking about? Do you think your tea was doped?"

"Oh, I know what's been going on," Mrs. Durham said. "Lola has been putting something in my tea. Something that makes me sleepy. I didn't mind, because I'm happier when I sleep. But she's been increasing it. I think she means to kill me."

176

Durham looked uncertain for just a second, then threw a hard look at Lola Marchant. "Is that true? By God, woman, if you—"

"Oh no you don't!" Lola snapped, and the muzzle of her revolver swung toward Durham. "I'm not taking the blame for what was your idea. You supplied the dope, whatever it is. Don't try passing the buck to me!"

"Why you dirty little bitch!" Durham snarled, taking a step toward Lola.

Lola's gun spoke, and Durham pulled up short, with an expression of stunned disbelief on his face. He wavered a moment, then crumpled to the floor, face down. There was a hole in the back of his night shirt where the bullet had exited, and judging from its location, the slug had passed through his heart.

Marshal Banks, surprising Harding with his speed reaction, reached Lola before anyone else recovered from the shock. He twisted the pistol out of her grasp and put in in his pocket.

"You're under arrest. Unless I miss my guess, the charge will be murder."

Lola shrugged, and gave him an odd smile. "It won't stick, Marshal. I shot in self-defense. All of you saw him coming at me." She smiled, and added confidently, "Besdies, you'd never get a jury to convict me."

Harding, remembering his conversation with Mazie Bowen, had to agree with her. It had been cold-blooded murder, but he doubted that Lola would be found guilty. Probably she would have some way of blackmailing at least one of the jurors. Besides, juries were notably loathe to convict a woman, especially a good-looking one.

Doc Mapes knelt down and rolled Durham onto his back. A red stain was spreading over Durham's night shirt. It didn't take an expert to know that the man was dead. The doctor straightened up and turned his attention to Lola Marchant.

"What have you been giving Mrs. Durham?"

"Don't ask me," Lola said carelessly. "Some kind of powder. Moose got it in Denver. He never told me what it was. By the way, if you'll look at his leg, you'll find another bullet hole. I bandaged it for him when he came in a few minutes ago."

After Doc Mapes had verified this, Harding looked at Banks.

"I guess that proves my point, Marshal. It was Durham who set off the blast under the barn."

Mrs. Durham moved shakily into the room and sat down on a chair. She looked at Harding.

"Do you mean that my husband caused the explosion? Was anybody hurt?"

"Yes," Harding said. "A young man named Billy Gregg. Chances are he'll recover. Unfortunately, I can't say the same for the building. It's a total loss." He smiled ruefully. 'It's pretty hard to collect damages from a dead man."

Mrs. Durham didn't answer, in fact Harding wasn't sure she had even been listening. He turned toward Marshal Banks.

"I guess you won't be needing me for anything. I'll go back and see how Billy's getting along."

Banks merely nodded, and Harding left the house. There was quite a group in front of the place. One of them, a man Harding didn't know, asked curiously, "What went on in there? We heard the gunshot."

"Lola Marchant killed Moose Durham," Harding said. "Marshal Banks will probably give you the details when he comes out." He elbowed his way through the group and headed for Dr. Mapes's office. A lot had happened in the last hour, and he needed time to digest it. One thing sure, the Feeney Freight Line was out of existence. Well, he had taken blows before; he could snap back from this one. Frisco, despite his tendency to grumble over minor irritations, would not complain.

What bothered Harding most was the effect on Molly Root and Spud Gagan. There wouldn't be many opportunities around Leadville for a girl with Molly's qualifications, and as for Spud Gagan, he was no longer a young man. He would probably have difficulty finding work. Billy, if his injuries weren't serious, would make out all right.

Both Molly and Frisco were in Dr. Mapes's office and, to Harding's great relief, Billy was sitting up on the edge of the table. To Harding's question, he replied that he was feeling all right except for a headache.

Molly looked inquiringly at Harding. "What happened at Moose Durham's house? We thought we heard a gunshot."

Harding nodded. "Durham is dead. Lola Marchant killed him."

And he went on to tell the rest of what had taken place. As he finished, Dr. Mapes came into the room. He looked at Billy Gregg, and smiled.

"So you're all right, are you? It must be nice to be young."

"I'm fine," Billy said. "Mr. Harding just told us what happened at Durham's house. I feel sort of sorry for Mrs. Durham."

"You needn't," Dr. Mapes said. "She'll probably get well, now that no one's doping her." He turned to Harding and added, "By the way, she wants to talk to you."

"To me? About what?"

"She didn't say," Doc answered. "But whatever it is, it'll have to wait until morning. I've given her something to let her sleep. No, not the stuff Lola's been putting in her tea. And now if you folks don't mind, I'll get a little rest.''

"We can take a hint," Harding said, smiling. "Billy, you'd better come to the boarding house. I'm sure Hetty Cook can fix you up with a place to bed down.''

"Yes, sir," Billy said, and the four of them left the office.

Chapter Twenty-Four

To nobody's surprise, Mrs. Cook found a place for Billy to spend the night. It was just a couch in the parlor but, as Billy pointed out, it was a lot more comfortable than a wagon bed. Molly bid them all good night and went to her room. Harding and Frisco were about to follow suit when there was a knock at the front door. Mrs. Cook opened it, and from outside came Marshal Banks's voice.

"Is Harding here?"

"Yes he is, Marshal. Won't you come in?"

"Thanks, but I'd rather talk to him out here."

Harding slanted a puzzled glance at Frisco and went out, not knowing what to expect. After some of the things which had happened lately, almost anything was possible. He was relieved at Banks's apologetic tone as he said, "Sorry to bother you, Harding, but something's come up that I think you ought to know, since it's liable to concern you as much as anyone. I'm afraid you aren't going to like it."

"Something new? I thought everything that could go wrong already had. What now?"

"Dobbs and Faraday are out of jail."

"Oh Lord!" Harding groaned. "I was hoping that with Durham no longer around to bail them out they'd be sent up for a long stretch. How come you turned them loose?"

"I didn't, dammit. They broke jail."

Frisco had followed Harding out in time to hear most of the conversation, and he now said sourly, "What've you got down there, a cracker box? I suppose they kicked a hole in the wall."

"No," Banks said. "But they managed to loosen one of the bars in the window and squeeze through. Nobody's ever escaped before. Of course nobody has tried very hard. I didn't expect Dobbs and Faraday to be any different. Hell, they was supposed to be turned loose as soon as the judge got back. I can't . . ."

"Wait a minute," Harding cut in, as a possible explanation occurred to him. "Suppose they found out about Durham being killed. They might have realized that without him to back them up, they'd be in real trouble." He looked at Banks. "Could anybody have told them?"

"I reckon so," the marshal said. "Half the town knew about it by the time I got back to my office. Almost anybody could've tipped 'em off. And what you said is likely true. Without Durham to go their bail, and then pay their fine and damages, they could've been in more trouble than they'd bargained for." He hesitated a moment, then added, "Which they would probably blame on you, being as it was you that got them in jail in the first place. That's why I thought you'd want to know."

"You're right," Harding said. "And now that we've been warned, we'd better do something about it." He looked around at Frisco, and added wryly, "Seems we're not out of the woods yet, partner. With those two polecats on the prowl, our lives aren't worth a plugged nickle. And I don't hanker to go around looking over my shoulder."

"Me neither," Frisco said. "So let's go find 'em."

"Later," Harding told him, and added before Frisco could protest, "We'll have a better chance of locating them in daylight. Besides which we've had a rough day.

What we need most right now is a good night's sleep."
He turned back to Dave Banks.

"I'm obliged to you, Marshal, for warning us. We'll
be seeing you first thing in the morning. Good night."

Sounding relieved, the marshal told them good night
and hurried away. Harding, sensing that Frisco was
about to explode, managed to get him to their room
before he could say anything. Once they were there,
Frisco blurted out, "What was all that hogwash about
letting things ride until morning? You know danged well
we ought to be looking for Dobbs and Faraday right this
minute."

"You're right," Harding agreed. "But I also know
that we don't want the marshal under our feet every step
we take, and I couldn't think of a better way to get rid
of him. Remember when we rented this room I said I
was glad the window was close to the ground?"

Frisco nodded without saying anything, and Harding
continued. "Now you see what I had in mind. How
would you like to take a moonlight stroll?"

"Why you tricky son of a gun!" Frisco said,
grinning. "For a minute there I thought you'd gone
loco. When do we start?"

"Right now," Harding said, and blew out the lamp.

Moments later they were outside, having opened and
closed the window as quietly as possible. After listening
a few minutes to make sure no one had heard them
leave, Harding touched Frisco's shoulder, and moved
off in the general direction of the Durham barn. It
seemed as good a place as any to start.

Although Harding had never visited the Rocky
Mountain Company's barn, he had of course seen it
from a distance, so he and Frisco were able to approach
it from the rear. There was an open area about fifty
yards wide around the building, and enough starlight so

that they would be clearly visible if anyone were watching for them. Harding motioned for Frisco to stop, and leaned close to whisper in his ear.

"You stay here and keep me covered. Don't follow until I'm out of the open."

Frisco nodded, and Harding took off, bending low and zigzagging to make a more elusive target. He reached the side of the barn safely, and stood in its shadow, but he didn't breathe easily until Frisco had joined him. His relief was combined with disappointment, for he felt that if Dobbs and Faraday were there, they would have made their presence known.

This feeling was substantiated when he and Frisco found a back door to the barn, entered quietly, and scouted the interior, finding only one human occupant, a man who was sleeping peacefully on some baled hay. Harding supposed that he had been left on guard, in which case he was not doing a good job of it. Possibly he already knew that Durham was dead, and felt that this relieved him of responsibility.

Outside again, and in the shelter of some trees, Harding said softly, "It looks like we've just wasted our time. I doubt if Dobbs and Faraday have even been here."

"So what do we do now?" Frisco asked, trying unsuccessfully to keep his voice low.

"In the first place," Harding said, "let me do the talking. You've got a good voice for hog calling, but not for something like this. To answer your question, I think our next best bet would be that shack where they live. I was there with the marshal and Guillford, and I think I can find it even in this dim light. Follow me, and don't talk unless you have to."

Frisco nodded, and Harding led off, skirting the backs of the business buildings in case anyone were still abroad on the main street. He had no difficulty finding the shack, which was dark, but something warned him against going to the door, even though the front of the house was in shadow, which would keep him and Frisco from being clearly visible. He couldn't explain the feeling, but he had learned to trust his instincts.

Motioning Frisco to stay where he was, Harding circled the shack and approached it from a side which was also in shadow. With his ear pressed against the thin wall, he listened intently. After perhaps five minutes he concluded that either the house was unoccupied, or Dobbs and Faraday were a lot more clever than he gave them credit for. He moved over to the one window on this side of the shack, opened it carefully, and slid over the sill. Still no challenge.

Convinced now that he was alone, Harding still couldn't shake the feeling of impending danger. Deciding to gamble, he drew his sixgun, struck a match which he cupped in his left hand, took a quick look around, and just as quickly snuffed out the match. What he had seen was enough to justify his hunch: a double-barreled shotgun fastened to a tabletop in such a way that its twin muzzles pointed at the door. He hadn't seen any wires or strings, but was satisfied that they were there. Grinning to himself, he gingerly turned the table so that the shotgun was no longer pointed at the door. With this accomplished, he left the house the same way he had entered, and rejoined Frisco.

There was no longer any particular need for silence, but Harding nevertheless kept his voice low as he said, "We're going in, and when we do, there's going to be a hell of a bang. Hit the floor, and have your gun ready, but don't say anything. Let's go!"

As he had promised, there was a deafening explosion when he pushed open the door. Harding flung himself

185

to one side and rolled over to face the doorway. He had enough confidence in Frisco to know that he would do the same.

For a minute the silence was absolute, partly on account of the deafening effect of the shotgun blast. Then there was the sound of footsteps out front, a shape loomed in the doorway, and Dobbs' voice said triumphantly, "Got 'em, by God! Now let's get out of here before Banks comes to see what made all the noise."

"Not so fast," Faraday said. "I want to be sure they're both dead. Light the lamp."

Dobbs grumbled, but his boots scraped on the wooden floor. A match flared, and Harding could see Dobbs bending down to light the lamp. Harding waited until it was lit, then said sharply, "Hold it, you two! You're both covered."

Dobbs gasped, but instead of obeying Harding's command, went for his gun. He had half turned when Harding's bullet caught him in the ribs, knocking him down. At the same time, Frisco's gun roared, and Faraday pitched sideways, his gun flying out of his hand. Neither man moved, but Harding didn't relax until he had recovered both their guns and tossed them into a corner of the room. At this, Dave Banks came charging through the doorway, his gun fisted. Harding, without giving Banks time for his customary "What's going on here?" said complacently, "We found your escaped prisoners, Marshal. As you can see, they had set a shotgun trap for us. Or for you, if you had happened to come first. I gave them a chance to drop their guns, but Dobbs was too stupid to take advantage of it, so Faraday had to try, too. If you have any questions or complaints, now's the time to make them."

"No questions," Banks said, and holstered his gun.

"In that case," Harding told him, "Frisco and I are

going home and go to bed. It's been a long day. Good night, Marshal.''

"Good night," Banks said, and watched silently as the two men stepped past the dead bodies and left.

Chapter Twenty-Five

The following morning, Harding awoke to find Frisco already up and dressed, and staring down at him impatiently.

"Thought you was going to sleep all day," Frisco grumbled.

"What time is it?"

"You know I ain't got a watch," Frisco said. "But I can smell food cooking, so I know we'd better get moving or we'll miss our breakfast."

Harding yawned, got out of bed, and pulled on his pants. He was in the midst of shaving when Frisco asked, "Now that we're out of business, what do you aim to do?"

"I haven't had time to think about it," Harding admitted. "The important thing is that we're both alive, no thanks to Moose Durham or his hired guns. And Molly and Billy are, too."

"Speaking of which," Frisco said, "I think they're in love. You should've seen the look on Molly's face when you carried Billy out of the burning barn."

"They'll make a good pair," Harding said. "Billy's got the stuff in him to go places, and Molly . . . well, if I were fifteen years younger, I'd give Billy a run for his money."

"Who're you trying to fool?" Frisco scoffed. "You're not the marrying kind. If you ever get hitched, it'll have to be to a gypsy."

"Could be you're right," Harding said. "But it isn't going to spoil my appetite. Let's go down and eat.

Afterwards, I'm supposed to go over to Durham's house. Doc told me Mrs. Durham wanted to see me."

When Harding knocked at the door, it was opened by Mrs. Durham herself, looking much better than Harding would have expected. She smiled, and motioned for him to enter.

"We can talk in the study, Mr. Harding. It'll be more comfortable there."

"Yes'm," Harding said, trying not to notice the bloodstains on the hall floor. Mrs. Durham preceded him into the study, where she seated herself behind Moose's desk, and motioned for Harding to take a chair.

"You're probably wondering why I sent for you."

Harding nodded. "I'll admit I'm a little curious. I would have thought you'd never want to see me again, after . . ." He left the sentence unfinished.

"On the contrary," Mrs. Durham said, "What I've heard about you made me realize that you're the one person who can do me some good. What are your plans, now that your place of business has gone up in smoke? Do you intend to start over again here in Leadville?"

"No, ma'am," Harding said. "My partner and I will take our losses and move on."

"If you accept my proposition, you won't have any losses, Mr. Harding. You see, I'm now sole owner of the Rocky Mountain Freighting Company. It's ironic, in a way; I'm sure my husband wouldn't have wanted it that way. He just never got around to making a will."

"Congratulations," Harding said sincerely. "You've inherited a good business."

"So I'm told," Mrs. Durham said. "But I'm not qualified to run it. I'd like to hire you to take charge. You and your partner."

This caught Harding by surprise.

"You hardly know me, Mrs. Durham. Don't you think you'd be taking a chance?"

"I'm not as foolish as my late husband let folks believe. I know what I'm doing. Oh, by the way, I intend to pay you for the loss of your barn and equipment." She raised a delicate hand to forestall a protest. "I can afford it, Mr. Harding. I've been looking over the books, and it seems that I'm going to be quite well fixed. What do you say? Will you do it?"

Thoughts had been racing through Harding's mind. It was really too good an offer to turn down. On the other hand . . .

"On two conditions, Mrs. Durham. My partner and I will take charge of the freighting company long enough to make sure it's operating smoothly. But you'll have to take Molly Root and Spud Gagan as part of the deal. Also Billy Gregg."

"That will be perfectly satisfactory."

"One more thing," Harding said. "When the business is running smoothly, Frisco and I will be free to leave."

Mrs. Durham frowned. "But I wanted to be sure the business was in good hands."

"Don't worry," Harding said. "It will be. Molly Root knows more about the office end of the operation than I do, and Billy Gregg will be able to run the actual freighting. You won't have anything to complain about, believe me."

"Well . . ." Mrs. Durham's smile returned. "If those are your terms, Mr. Harding, I accept. Do we need something in writing?"

"I don't," Harding said. He reached across the desk. "We can just shake hands on it."

"Very well," Mrs. Durham said, placing her small

hand in his big one.

Feeling a trifle giddy, Harding left the house. He found Frisco, Molly, and Billy looking at the rubble of the barn. The horses had been placed in the livery stable.

"You aren't going to believe this," Harding said. "But Mrs. Durham just hired all of us to work for Rocky Mountain Freighting Company."

"The blazes you say!" Frisco exclaimed. "Does that mean that we're going to be stuck in this North Pole climate indefinitely?"

"No," Harding assured him. "As soon as we have things running properly, you and I will be free to pull out, leaving it up to Molly and Billy to run the outfit." He looked at Molly. "Providing you're agreeable, that is."

Molly and Billy exchanged glances, and apparently they understood each other, for Molly said, "We're agreeable." Billy merely grinned and nodded.

"Good," Harding said. "So let's get started. If we work hard, we may have things in shape before Christmas." He turned to grin at Frisco. "I know you've been looking forward to spending the holidays making snowmen here in Leadville, but you'll just have to force yourself to leave. Okay, partner?"

"Damn betcha!" Frisco said. "You know something? I'm beginning to feel warmer already."

ZANE GREY'S ARIZONA AMES:
Gun Trouble in Tonto Basin
Romer Zane Grey

PRICE: $1.95 BT51479
CATEGORY: Western

GUN TROUBLE IN TONTO BASIN marks the reappearance of one of Zane Grey's most memorable characters, Arizona Ames. Young Rich Ames leads the life of a range drifter after a gunfight that leaves two men dead, and his skill earns him a reputation as one of the fastest guns in the West. Then, Arizona Ames comes home to find his range and his family haunted by the shadow of a terror they dare not name!

This is the third in a series of westerns based on characters created by Zane Grey, Romer Zane Grey's famous father. Among the other Zane Grey characters you will meet in this series are: LARAMIE NELSON, YAQUI, NAVADA JIM LACY and BUCK DUANE.